She could tell there was something wrong. . . .

"Lisa," Talli said to her best friend, "are you okay?"

"Dandy," Lisa replied. "Never been better." She turned toward Talli with a bright smile. "Fooled you, didn't I?" Her curly brown hair straightened and became straw-yellow, her eyes lightened, and her face lengthened.

"Pretty damn good, huh?" the vampire asked. "Haven't figured out how to walk yet, though. And voices—man, are voices hard to do. But give me another day to practice, and I'll fool her mother." There was a snapping and popping as muscle and bone shifted on his frame. Lisa's sweater stretched as his shoulders widened.

Talli backed away in horror. "Where is Lisa?" she demanded.

"Gone, gone, gone," the vampire said. He made a sound like someone slurping a milk shake through a straw. "Just another midnight snack."

Don't miss the other two books in this
terrifying trilogy

*The Substitute**
*The Coach**

Read these thrillers
from HarperPaperbacks!

Babysitter's Nightmare
Sweet Dreams
Sweetheart
Teen Idol
Running Scared
by Kate Daniel

And look for

Class Trip
by Bebe Faas Rice

* coming soon

THE PRINCIPAL

M. C. Sumner

HarperPaperbacks
A Division of HarperCollins*Publishers*

This is a work of fiction. The characters, incidents, and dialogues are products of the author's imagination and are not to be construed as real. Any resemblance to actual events or persons, living or dead, is entirely coincidental.

HarperPaperbacks *A Division of* HarperCollins*Publishers*
10 East 53rd Street, New York, N.Y. 10022

Copyright © 1994 by Mark C. Sumner and
Daniel Weiss Associates, Inc.

Cover art copyright © 1994 Daniel Weiss Associates, Inc.

All rights reserved. No part of this book may be used or reproduced in any manner whatsoever without written permission of the publisher, except in the case of brief quotations embodied in critical articles and reviews. For information address Daniel Weiss Associates, Inc., 33 West 17th Street, New York, New York 10011.

Produced by Daniel Weiss Associates, Inc., 33 West 17th Street, New York, New York 10011.

First printing: February, 1994

Printed in the United States of America

HarperPaperbacks and colophon are trademarks of HarperCollins*Publishers*

10 9 8 7 6 5 4 3 2 1

For the people of Greenville, Kentucky. I borrowed some of the town's geography when constructing the fictional Westerberg, but the real Greenville is altogether prettier, nicer, and has much better schools.

And for my cousins Emily and Jessica, who said nice things about my last book.

Prologue

❧

The old man opened the door to the school and stepped inside. The door closed behind him, cutting off the sunlight that spilled in from outside. He stood for a moment in the gloom of the entryway, then began to walk slowly down the hall.

He had gone no more than ten steps when a loud bell rang. Within seconds, doors up and down the hallway flew open, and students spilled out. The old man stepped to the side as the first of the students went hurrying past.

The noise in the hallway was deafening—students were talking, yelling, running, arguing. A thousand metal locker doors squeaked open as books were thrown in. The old man saw a boy in a black leather jacket grab a girl by the arm and pull her out of the traffic. He thought at first that they were going to kiss, but the boy twisted the girl's arm behind her back and pressed his face close to hers, his lips snarling in anger. The girl tried to turn away, tears leaking from the corners of her eyes. The old man smiled.

A group of students wearing denim jackets with the sleeves torn off sauntered by. They were laughing, but it was a mean, bitter kind of laugh. One of the boys in the group pulled back the bottom of his jacket just enough for the plastic grip of a cheap pistol to show. The other boys in the group laughed louder, and the old man joined in, but no one looked his way.

None of the students seemed to notice him as they streamed past. He watched them all, his pale eyes taking in a thousand faces, his smile growing wider every second. He reached out and let his long thin fingers trail through the curly red hair of a girl walking by.

Immediately the color drained from her face. She stumbled, and her books went spilling across the floor. Looking confused, she knelt to pick up her things. As she did, a boy with pale hair stopped to look at her. With a sneer on his thin face, he booted one of the books far down the hall. The girl looked up and shouted something as the blond boy walked away, but the old man wasn't paying attention to her. He was watching the blond boy closely. He wanted to be sure he remembered this one.

When the flow of students had thinned to a trickle, the man pushed himself from the wall. Walking much more briskly than he had when entering the school, the man made his way toward the principal's office. He stopped in front of a row of glass windows and stared in at a woman typing slowly on an ancient typewriter.

The woman pulled out a page of paper and walked over to a battered metal file cabinet. While she sorted through the folders in the top drawer of the cabinet, the old man stepped into the office and walked past her. There was a door at the other end of the office. On it was a small brass plaque that said OLIVER SHAY, PRINCIPAL. The old man opened the door without knocking and stepped through, closing the door behind him.

The middle-aged man behind the desk wore thick glasses, and the brown hair on top of his head was thinning to show a bit of pink scalp. He hunched forward in his chair, scribbling on one of the forms that were heaped on his desk.

There was only one other chair in the room, and the old man settled into it. He waited for a few seconds, studying the man behind the desk. Then he cleared his throat.

The man behind the desk looked up, startled. "I'm sorry," he said. "I didn't hear you come in."

"That's quite all right," said the old man. "I take it you're the principal?"

"That's right," the man agreed. He stood up

and came around the desk with his hand extended. "Oliver Shay," he said.

The old man took his hand in a dry grip. "I want to ask you a few questions, Mr. Shay."

The principal smiled. "Oliver, please." He released the old man's hand and went back to his chair. "Are you here about one of our students, Mr. . . . ?"

"I'm here about all of your students," said the old man. He folded his long hands into his lap. "This school is in trouble."

Mr. Shay's smile dimmed. "I'm sorry," he said. "Who did you say you are?"

"Someone who's going to change the direction of this school," said the old man.

"Are you from the state education department?" Mr. Shay asked.

"Who I am is not important." The old man leaned back in his chair. "Tell me, Mr. Shay, do you find this job very stimulating? Working with all these young people?"

Mr. Shay's dark eyebrows were knit together in confusion. "I'm afraid I don't know what you're after. If you would only tell me who you are . . ."

"All these young people," the old man repeated. He shook his head and smiled slightly. "They're so tempting, aren't they?"

Mr. Shay's hand went to the phone on his desk. "I'm going to ask you to leave," he said. His fingers jabbed at the buttons on the phone.

4

The old man stood up suddenly. His chair fell over, thumping against the short carpet. "No more time for games," he said sharply. His arm snaked out and he pulled the phone from Mr. Shay's grip. Before the principal could make another move, the old man had stepped around the desk. His left hand came up and his long fingers went around Mr. Shay's throat.

The principal's eyes bulged from their sockets. His glasses fell from his face and clattered to the floor.

"There are a few questions I need answered, Mr. Shay," said the old man. "It won't take very long." He smiled again. "Not long at all."

Ten minutes later, the door to the office opened and the old man came out. He dropped a piece of paper on the desk in front of the woman as he passed. She did not look up.

5

One

Tuesday

There was red paint splashed across Talli's locker. The stain ran down the green wall and made bright blood-colored puddles on the scuffed tile floor. There were too many people in the way for Talli to see if the spray-paint artist had been writing something, or just out to make a mess. She sighed, and did her best to open the locker without getting the paint on her hands.

The hallway was so crowded that opening the locker meant someone had to move, which no one seemed happy to do. Talli managed to shove in her math book while making a grab for her science book. As she did, a paperback slid out and thumped to the floor.

"Another horror novel, McAlister?" asked a voice at her back.

Talli twisted her head around to see Lisa Taylor grinning down at her. "Can you reach it?" Talli asked. "I'm crammed in here so tight that I can't even bend down."

"Okay. You can't get out, I can't get in," Lisa said. "I get your gory novel. You get my chemistry book out of my locker. Deal?"

"Deal," Talli said. "If I can get to it. What's your combination?"

"I don't have a combination anymore. Somebody smashed the lock off last week. They didn't take anything—I guess schoolbooks aren't worth much."

"Oh, that's wonderful." Talli reached between two other students to grab the handle of Lisa's locker. She felt inside and came out with the thick chemistry book. As she handed it to Lisa, she noticed a red stain on her sleeve. "Great," she said. "Another glorious day at Westerberg High."

Lisa took the science book. "At least it's red paint."

"Is that good?"

"Sure. It matches your hair." She passed the paperback over to Talli. "There's a little paint on this, too. But it looks like a book that *should* be dripping blood. What is this one? Werewolves?"

"Ghosts," Talli said. She tossed the book

7

back into her locker and closed the door. "It's not bad."

"I don't know," Lisa said. "After that one you gave me to read, I was scared to—" The bell sounded, cutting off Lisa's words. The jostling and bumping in the hallway picked up.

"Come on," Talli said as soon as the ringing stopped. "We better get to class." Lisa nodded, turned, and began pushing her way down the hall. Talli followed behind, staying as close as she could to her friend's bouncing brown ponytail.

From Talli's point of view, the hallway was an unending series of hunched shoulders and arms loaded with books. She hoped that Lisa, who was a good four inches taller than she, could see where she was going.

A guy with a red bandanna dangling from the back pocket of his jeans cut in front of Talli. The year before, Talli wouldn't have thought a thing about it. Now she knew that the bandanna was probably a signal that he was selling drugs. She still had a hard time believing that this was the same high school she'd gone to for three years. Last year she had breezed through these hallways without having to fight crowds. There had never been graffiti on the wall. If someone had smashed open Lisa's locker, it would have merited a full-scale investigation by the principal.

That was before Cushing High had been

closed. All those budget numbers in the paper that had seemed as cold and remote as the far side of the moon now meant that Westerberg High was crammed with all the high school students in the district. Even in a small town, that meant a lot of kids. Classes that had been comfortable at twenty or thirty students now had forty, fifty—even sixty. Some of the teachers were still trying, but managing such large classes was nearly impossible. A lot of them had just given up.

The final bell was ringing as Talli and Lisa slipped through the door. Naturally the only seats open were in the front rows. Talli took a seat in the front, and Lisa dropped into the desk behind her. Talli was glad that she had a seat. Some classrooms were so short of desks that latecomers had to stand or sit on the floor.

The teacher, Ms. Solomon, had just finished sketching a diagram on the chalkboard when the intercom began to crackle. Everyone paused, waiting for the message.

"Attention, all teachers and students," said a woman's voice. "As of last night, Principal Shay has resigned from his duties at Westerberg High School."

This brought a few chuckles from the back of the room, and someone gave a loud cheer.

"Be quiet," Ms. Solomon said.

Talli wasn't surprised. At the last school-board meeting, Mr. Shay had been under attack from all sides. Talli had a lot of respect for the principal, and she was really sorry to see him go. But she had to admit that he hadn't been very good at controlling all the problems around the school.

There was another squawk of static, then the voice on the intercom started again. "It may be several weeks before a new principal is selected by the school board. In the meantime, Mr. Henry Volker has been appointed our interim principal. He will be assisted by Mr. Avram Lynch. All teachers are asked to stay after school today. Thank you." There was a final squeal from the speaker, then everyone in the room started talking at once.

"Good riddance," said a guy two seats over from Talli.

Lisa leaned forward. "Maybe this Volker guy will clean things up."

"I don't think so," Talli said, twisting around to look at her friend.

"Why not?"

"Because I've already met him."

"You knew we were getting a new principal?" Lisa asked.

"No," Talli replied. "Mr. Volker is renting a house a couple of doors down from me. I met him when he moved in, but I didn't know he was going to be our new principal."

"Ooh, neighbors with the principal. That should be real fun." Lisa smiled. "So what's he like? A mega-jerk?"

"No. He's just—"

"Back to work, everyone," Ms. Solomon said. "I know it's exciting news, and if we get through our lesson, we can discuss it at the end of class."

The noise slacked off, and Talli turned back around. There wasn't much chance they would finish the lesson—classes were so unruly that none of the teachers ever got through a whole lesson.

"He's what?" prompted Lisa softly.

Talli leaned her head back. "He's old," she whispered. "Really old."

"Great," Lisa said. "We need a marine and they send us a geriatric."

"Lisa Taylor. Talli McAlister. Are you finished with your conversation now?" Ms. Solomon stood over them with her hands on her hips.

"Yeah," Lisa said.

Ms. Solomon went back the chalkboard, and Talli struggled to pay attention. By the time the bell rang, Talli had filled four pages of her notebook.

Lisa started to get up, but Talli put a hand on her shoulder. "Let's wait," she said. Talli stayed in her chair as the rest of the students hurried into the hall. "At least we won't have to fight the flood," she said.

"The best thing about helping with the play this year," Lisa said, "is getting into that big empty auditorium." She looked at the students

11

flowing past the door and wrinkled her nose. "This place is starting to give me claustrophobia." She stood and carefully arranged her purse so that it hung under her arm. A lot of girls had already lost purses to thieves who easily disappeared into the crush of students.

The warning bell rang, and students began to trickle in for Ms. Solomon's next class. "Let's get going," Talli said.

As they stepped through the door, a familiar face topped with unruly dark hair appeared. Alex Cole looked at them in surprise for a moment, then his face broke into a crooked smile. "Hi, Talli."

"Uh, maybe I'll go on and you can catch up," Lisa said.

"No," Talli said firmly. "I'm right behind you."

"Talli," Alex said again. "Can I just talk to you for a minute?"

She looked at him through narrowed eyes. "You didn't seem that interested in talking to me Friday night. You were more interested in going to a ball game with your friends than keeping a date with me."

"But all the guys were going to that game," he protested. His dark blue eyes looked very sincere. "It's really hard to get in, and Rick had free tickets, so I thought . . ."

"Well, you can take Rick out *next* Friday night too," Talli said. "Come on, Lisa." She headed out the door without looking back.

"You know you're going to forgive him," Lisa said as they fought their way down the hall.

"What makes you think so?"

"You always do. You two have been together since third grade. You wouldn't know what to do with yourself if you didn't have Alex to argue with."

Talli tried to keep a stern look on her face, but she couldn't fight back a smile. "Are we really that obvious?"

"I've seen you two do this so often, I could make up the words myself." Lisa paused by the double doors to the auditorium. "Why don't you guys just skip the fighting and concentrate on the good stuff?"

"Because the fighting keeps the good stuff good," Talli said. She pushed open one of the doors, and they stepped into the cool, empty auditorium. As soon as the doors closed behind them, the noise of the crowded hallways faded to a low hum.

"I really love this place," Lisa said.

"Me, too," Talli replied. "But I wish they had spent less money giving us a fancy theater and gym and used more of it to keep Cushing High open."

"I hear you." Lisa dropped her books onto a seat in the first row, and Talli did the same. "So, what's on the agenda for today, stage manager number one?"

13

"Scenery painting, stage manager number two," Talli said. "More castle pieces for *Hamlet*."

They mounted the steps at the side of the stage and headed for the scenery storage room. Halfway across the stage, Lisa paused and turned toward the empty seats. "You ever think about being in the play instead of behind the scenes?"

"Not me," Talli said. "I hate talking in front of people." She walked through the dark corridor that ran behind the stage and opened the door to the prop room.

Talli took one look into the room and froze in sudden terror.

Two

❧❧❧

There were three guys sitting on the floor of the
room. A small stack of plastic Baggies lay on the
floor between them. One of the guys had his
hand extended, a fat wad of cash jutting from
his fingers. All three were looking at Talli.

"You need something, baby?" asked the nearest of the three.

"No, I . . ." Talli took a half-step backward. "I
just . . ."

Lisa bumped into her from behind. "What's
wrong?" she asked. Then she peered over Talli's
shoulders. "Uh-oh," she said.

The guy who had spoken to Talli got to his
feet and walked over to the door. He was tall,
with dark hair pulled into a ponytail, and a col-
orful tattoo peeking from the neck of his white
T-shirt. "You looking for some action?" he asked.

15

"Is there anything you ladies need?"

"We're leaving," Lisa said. She took Talli by the arm. "Come on."

The guy took a quick step forward and caught Talli by the other arm. "I don't think you ought to leave yet." His eyes swept from the top of Talli's head down to her legs, and back up to her eyes. "This is a nice quiet place. Why don't you two spend a little time with us? We need the company."

"Yeah," said another of the guys. "Come in and keep us company." All three of them laughed.

Talli pulled her arms free. "We can't," she said. "We have to get back to class."

"They won't miss you," said the second guy. He was shorter than the first, but wider. He got up and joined the guy who had grabbed Talli at the door. "We'd miss you, though. Stay with us."

"Come on," Lisa said. "Let's get out of here." She turned away from the prop room and took a step back into the darkness. As she did, the first guy pushed past Talli and grabbed Lisa by both shoulders. He spun her around savagely.

He leaned over and put his face only an inch away from Lisa's. "You wouldn't be going to tell anyone what you saw here, would you?" he asked.

"Let her go!" Talli shouted. The bare arm of the shorter guy snaked around her neck.

"Don't you tell us what to do," he whispered in Talli's ear.

"We won't say anything," Lisa said. "Just let us go, and we'll forget you were ever here."

"That ain't good enough," said the one with the ponytail. He took Lisa's arm and pulled her back toward the prop room. "Let's sit down and talk about it. Maybe we can have some fun together."

Talli felt herself being turned. The arm across her throat was too tight even to think about fighting. The third guy was still sitting in the prop room. He was very skinny and had yellow hair that spilled like loose straw across his pale face. As Talli and Lisa were pushed toward him, he began to laugh.

"Is there a problem here?" asked a voice.

The ponytailed guy spun around and squinted as he peered into the darkness. "Go away," he said. "We got everybody we want."

"I see," said the voice. It was a soft voice, as clipped and dry as something from an old movie. "I think it would be best if you let the young ladies go." Talli twisted around, trying to see who was speaking, but she saw only the empty black corridor.

The guy holding Talli shoved her into the prop room. She spun around to see him slide a knife from inside his shirt.

There was a click of metal, and another knife appeared in the hand of the one with the ponytail. "Get out of here, you—"

Something moved through the corridor; a

17

streak of gray that darted forward, dashed the knife away, and moved back into the darkness. The ponytailed guy looked around wildly.

"Put down your weapons," the voice ordered.

"Who's there?" asked the guy with the ponytail. "Who are you?" Talli could hear a sudden shakiness in his voice.

"If you let the young ladies go, and relinquish the knives, you can still get out of this without getting hurt." The voice was unchanged, still soft and calm. Even though the owner of that voice seemed to be trying to help her, something about it made Talli shiver.

"Let's get him," said the shorter guy. "He can't take us both." But before he could move, there was a rush of air, and he grunted. The knife flew from his hand and went clattering off into the darkness. He stepped forward, then came flying back. He landed on the floor, moaning and clutching his stomach.

The ponytailed guy jumped to his right and lashed out with a closed fist. There was a sharp crack, as if he had struck his knuckles against a piece of wood. He screamed and drew back his hand.

Before he had a chance to recover, a hand slipped from the darkness and shoved him against the wall with such force that the plaster cracked. The ponytailed guy slid down the wall and lay sprawled half in and half out of the darkness.

"Are you ladies all right?" asked the voice.

Talli nodded numbly.

"Yes," Lisa said. "I think so." She rubbed her arm where the guy had grabbed her. "Thanks for taking care of those jerks."

A tall form stepped out of the shadows. The light from the prop room spilled over the sharp angles of a long, narrow face and shone on silver hair. "It is my job to help," said the tall man. "I am Mr. Volker, your new principal."

Lisa stepped toward him and held out her hand. "Hi, I'm Lisa Taylor."

Volker's long fingers closed around Lisa's hand and gave it a single shake. His narrow face turned to Talli. "I know you," he said. "You are the policeman's daughter. McAlister." He stepped over to her and looked down with a tight smile.

"Yes," Talli said. "Tallibeth McAlister." Volker gave her hand the same quick shake he had given Lisa. As his fingers pulled away from hers, Talli had the strangest feeling—a thrill of revulsion that jarred her from head to toe. It wasn't the first time she had had this feeling lately. She closed her eyes for a moment and shook her head, trying to clear it.

Volker was still staring at her when she opened her eyes.

"Tallibeth," he said. "That's quite an unusual name. I will remember it."

The laughter from the prop room rose in pitch. Talli turned and saw the yellow-haired guy still sitting beside the Baggies of drugs. His hair was down over his face, and he rocked back and forth on his folded legs.

"This gentleman appears to have taken too much of his own concoctions," Volker said. He turned his head toward the darkness. "Mr. Lynch!"

Another figure appeared from the corridor. He was shorter than Volker, but not by much, and his shoulders were so wide that Talli wondered if he would fit through the door. He was a young man, with shoulder-length sandy hair and a long, drooping mustache. The sleeves of his suit coat bulged over massive arms. His eyes were as gray as heavy fog.

"You want me, sir?" Lynch's voice was raspy and high, not at all what Talli would have expected from his appearance. There was a slight accent in it. British? German? It was too faint for Talli to tell.

"Mr. Lynch, will you assist these three young men to the detention center? I must go and call the police." He gave Talli another of his thin smiles. "Perhaps Ms. McAlister's father will be the one to clean up this mess for us."

Lynch grabbed the ponytailed guy by his shirt with one hand and lifted him to his feet. The student swayed, but he stayed standing. "To the office," Lynch said. When the guy didn't move, Lynch gave him a shove. The shorter guy was on his feet as soon as Lynch turned his way.

"I'm moving. I'm moving, okay?"

"To the office," Lynch said, "and don't try to get away."

"What about us?" Lisa asked. "Do we need to come to the office too?"

"Perhaps later," Volker said. "For now, I don't think you will have any more trouble here." He went to the door of the prop room. "Come with me," he said to the guy on the floor.

Still giggling, the guy gathered up the Baggies and followed Volker back down the dark hallway. Talli could hear him laughing all the way back through the auditorium.

"Wow," Lisa said as the door at the top of the auditorium swung shut. "I thought you said Volker was old."

"He is old," Talli said.

"Yeah, but you made it sound like he was in a wheelchair or something."

Talli shrugged. "He wasn't like this when I met him before. He was kind of stooped over, and he seemed . . . I don't know. Tired, I guess."

"Well, he sure wasn't tired today," Lisa said. "Did you see how he took those guys down? He was incredible."

"Yes," Talli said softly, looking up the dark hallway. "He was."

"And Lynch looks like he could pick up a school bus. Wait till everyone sees him. Half these stupid guys who think they're so tough will be scared to death of Lynch."

"I guess."

Lisa smiled. "This new principal is just what this place needs."

"I hope so," Talli said.

"What's wrong? You sound like you don't trust Volker. He just saved your neck." Lisa looked at Talli with lowered eyebrows. "And who knows what else he saved?"

"I know, it's just that . . ." Talli stopped and put her arms around herself. She couldn't shake the strange feeling that had come over her when Volker shook her hand. "I don't know." She turned back toward the prop room. "Come on, we better get painting, or Hamlet will be doing his soliloquy on a bare stage."

"Well, I think Volker is great," Lisa said. "And Lynch is even kind of cute."

Talli didn't answer.

Three

❧❧❧

If there was anyplace more crowded than the hallways of Westerberg High, it was the parking lot. Talli and Lisa stood shivering under the awning at the side of the school and watched people dashing to their cars through the cold, driving rain. Even though she had arrived twenty minutes early that morning, Talli was parked in a makeshift gravel lot more than five hundred yards from the door. Five hundred yards of puddles and gray mud.

"I don't suppose you have an umbrella?" Lisa asked.

"Sure I do," Talli said.

"Well, that's something. At least we—"

"I left it in the car," interrupted Talli.

"Oh." Lisa slid a notebook from her bag and held it over her hair. "We might as well

23

go. I don't think it's going to stop."

A hand came down on Talli's shoulder. "There you are!" Talli turned to see Samantha Deveraux smiling at her. "I've been looking all over for you."

"You were looking for me, Sam?" Talli asked. She knew Samantha hated to be called Sam. In Talli's book, that was reason enough to do it.

But Samantha didn't react to the nickname. "There's going to be a special school-board meeting tonight," she said. "You need to be there."

"Why?"

"For the student council, of course," Samantha said. She tossed her mane of blond hair.

"Sam, you're the student-council representative, not me," Talli said. "Why don't you go?"

Samantha made a little noise of surprise. "I have to be somewhere, okay?" She planted her hands on hips that were barely covered by a very short skirt.

"I've been at every school-board meeting this year," Talli told her. "The only one you went to was the time you knew the local TV would be there."

"Just do it," Samantha said. She threw her bright red purse over her shoulder, pivoted on her too-high heels, and wiggled back into the school, her long legs squeezed by the tight skirt.

"If she had any brains, she'd be dangerous," Talli said as the door closed behind Samantha.

"I hate her," Lisa said. Talli was startled by the emotion in her friend's voice.

"Hate Samantha? Why?"

Lisa raised an eyebrow. "You mean other than the fact that she's gorgeous? That all the guys hang around waiting for an excuse to drool all over her? That she treats every other girl in the school like dirt?" She planted her hands on her hips and tossed her head in imitation of Samantha. "That her hair doesn't even have the decency to frizz up in the rain?"

Talli smiled. "Yeah, besides that."

"I hate her for what she did to you," Lisa said. "You worked yourself to death on the student council. Along comes Ms. Legs-Up-to-Her-Neck, and you're out on your rear. I think all the guys voted for her just to make sure there was another picture of her in the yearbook."

"I'm still on the council."

"As an alternate. You do all the work, and Samantha gets all the credit."

A car drove by, splashing muddy water onto the sidewalk.

"Come on," Talli said. "Let's get out of here before it gets any worse."

Lisa put her notebook back over her brown curls. Talli just ran for it. She stepped in a puddle halfway across the gravel lot, and cold water poured into her sneaker. Samantha's hair might hold up to rain, but Talli's didn't. By the time they reached Talli's old orange Pinto, her bangs

25

were matted against her face in tight red ringlets. She fished her keys from her purse and started to open the door. The lock was sticky, and it took quite a bit of jiggling before it consented to open.

"Talli!"

Talli turned to see Alex running across the parking lot, splashing through the gray puddles.

"Is everybody going to try to talk to you in the parking lot?" Lisa asked.

"It looks that way," Talli said as she watched Alex approach.

"Give me the keys," Lisa said. "At least I can get in out of the rain while you two are going at it."

"This will only take a second."

"Sure it will." Lisa plucked the keys from Talli's hand and unlocked her door. "If you don't mind, I'll wait in here while you take your second." She climbed into the car and shut the door.

Alex came running up with his breath steaming in the cold, wet air. "I need to talk to you," he said.

"Alex, it's miserable out here," Talli said. "Can't this wait till later?"

He looked down at the muddy ground. "I just . . . I mean, I already said I was sorry." He turned his pleading blue eyes to Talli.

"You never said you were sorry," Talli said.

"I didn't?"

26

"No. You didn't."

"I'm sorry." Alex smiled his off-center smile. Rain ran down his forehead across his cheek, and dripped from his chin.

"Forgive me?"

Talli opened her mouth, closed it, and scowled at Alex. "You're not getting off that easy."

"Movie?" he asked.

"What kind of movie?"

"There's this new action movie playing down at the—"

"Excuse me," Talli said. She reached for the car door. "I'll be going now. Nice knowing you."

"Okay, okay! Horror triple feature over at the old Hammer Drive-In?"

Talli turned back to him with an appraising look. "Hmm, maybe you do love me after all." She waited a moment, then smiled. "Okay, I guess I'll take you back."

"Awfully generous of you," Alex said.

"Don't you forget it," Talli said. She leaned forward and gave him a quick kiss. He tasted like the rain. "Let's get out of this muck, and I'll call you from home. Okay?"

"You got it." His smile faded. He reached out and pushed a lock of Talli's damp hair back from her forehead. "I really am sorry."

She took his hand and held it for a second. "Okay, you really are forgiven. But if we don't get out of this rain, we'll both come down with pneumonia, and then I won't get my horror movies. Then you'll really be sorry."

"Bye!" Alex said. He turned and dashed back across the muddy parking lot. Talli hardly noticed the rain as she watched him go.

"All settled?" Lisa asked as Talli climbed into the car.

"Yup," Talli said. "Horror triple feature. All the popcorn I can eat." She cranked the car and shoved the gearshift into reverse.

"Sometimes I think you live on popcorn," Lisa said.

"Delicious and nutritious," Talli replied.

"And fattening," Lisa said. "At least the way they make it at the theater, it is." She clutched at her book bag as the car bounced over a pothole and out onto the street. "Of course, you never seem to have a problem with that." She sighed dramatically. "Unlike some of us."

"Lisa, you are not fat."

"Easy for you to say." Lisa turned toward her rain-streaked window as Talli steered through the wet town. The heavy rain had stripped the last brown autumn leaves from the trees, giving everything a look of winter. Though it was only afternoon, the low clouds and mist swallowed the light and made it seem like evening. Talli turned the headlights on as she turned onto the main highway and headed into the heart of Westerberg.

No matter what the latest census figures

28

might say, it was still a small town. A recent burst of growth had left it with a batch of shopping centers and fast-food places around the edges, but Westerberg was one of the few towns Talli had seen where downtown was still the place most people went to shop. The small stores were crowded together in buildings a hundred years old. Store windows were still colored by Halloween scenes painted by the grade-school kids. In front of the marble pillars of the old county courthouse, men were at work on the platform that would soon hold a huge Christmas tree cut from the woods outside of town.

Talli relaxed. As bad as the school had become, the town was as calm as ever. She loved it here, she always had. A lot of her friends complained that Westerberg was backward and boring. They always said there was nothing to do. Talli never understood them. She had Alex, she had her books, and she had her movies. What more could she want?

It was hard to believe a town like this would have a school as rough as Westerberg High. The school board kept saying that they were going to find the money to build a new, bigger school. She hoped they were telling the truth.

Lisa tapped her finger against the window. "My turn's coming up, don't miss it."

"I won't."

"Just making sure. You seemed like you were a million miles away."

"I'm paying attention," Talli said. "I was looking at the town."

"It looks scary," Lisa said softly.

"What does?" Talli asked.

"The town. Everything."

"What makes you say that?"

Lisa shrugged. "All these old buildings and bare trees. It looks like the cover on one of your spooky books."

"I guess it does look a little gloomy," Talli said, "but that's just the rain." She turned off the road and into the driveway of Lisa's house.

"I guess," Lisa said. She brightened as she opened her door and started to get out. "At least we have a new principal."

"Yeah."

"You coming by in the morning?"

"Absolutely," Talli said. "I'll be by right on time."

"Okay," Lisa said. "Have fun at the meeting." She slammed the door, and Talli watched her dash through the rain to her front door.

Talli pulled back onto the road and headed for home. In Westerberg, no place was too far from any other, and she went only a few blocks before turning onto her own street. She slowed as she passed the two-story white house that Principal Volker was renting. Talli remembered what Lisa said about the town looking like the cover of one of her horror novels.

She didn't think it was true of the town, but

it was certainly true of Volker's house. With its long dark windows bare of curtains, and no lights on, the house looked as empty as it had for the months before Volker rented it. The tall hedges and fences that surrounded the house hid the lower story and made it seem even more mysterious.

Talli drove past Volker's house and slid her car into her own driveway. As she climbed out of the car, the rain turned from a downpour to a deluge. Talli ran for the house with the cold rain soaking through her coat. She had her hand on the doorknob before she remembered the umbrella that was still sitting in the car.

As she opened the front door, Talli almost ran headlong into her father. "Dad, hi!" she said.

Her father raised a finger to his lips. "Shh," he said. He looked around for a second, then took Talli's hand and guided her over to the couch. "I don't want to frighten your mother," he whispered.

"About what?" Talli asked.

"About what happened at school," he said. "I got a call from the office. They said someone pulled a knife on you today. Is that true?"

"Yeah, I guess so. But I wasn't hurt or anything."

Her father cursed under his breath. "That's not the point. You *could* have been hurt. Howard tells me this new principal they've got stopped the jerks that were after you. Is that true?"

Talli nodded. "He knocked the knives away and took out all three of them."

"Three?" Her father's forehead creased. "Howard said there were two, but then Howard never got anything right in his life."

"There were two that had knives. I don't think the third guy even knew where he was."

"Drugs?"

"Yeah."

He shook his head and ran his strong fingers through his thick, iron-gray hair. "I'm really sorry it's like this for you, Talli. Your mother and I moved back down here when you were little because we thought this would be a good place for you to grow up. Now it's just as bad as anywhere in the city."

Footsteps sounded from the wood floor of the hallway, and Talli's mother stuck her head into the room. "What are you two doing in here?" she asked.

Talli smiled at her. "Nothing, Mom." She stood up. "I've got to eat a quick supper. There's a school-board meeting tonight."

"On a Tuesday? I thought the board always met on Thursday nights."

"This is a special meeting," Talli said.

"Well, I just got home from work myself," Mrs. McAlister said. "Get ready, and I'll see if there's anything to eat in this place." She turned and headed back down the hall.

"I've got to go pack," said her father. "I'll

probably be leaving about the same time you do."

"Still going to your conference?" Talli asked.

He nodded. "Can't get out of it. The state's requiring everyone to come in for this training, and it's my turn. Sheriff Bolger's going too." He put his big hand on her shoulder and squeezed. "You sure you're okay?"

"Yeah," Talli said. "I'm fine."

"I hate to be leaving now. If you have any more trouble, you go right to this new principal. The guys at the station all seem to be pretty impressed with him."

"I will," Talli said. But even as she smiled at her father, Talli knew she wouldn't go to Principal Volker, no matter what happened.

A bowl of soup made Talli feel warm on the inside, and after drying her hair and getting into some dry clothes, she felt presentable again. By the time she was ready to leave for the school-board meeting, her father was standing by the front door with a suitcase.

"Come on," he said. "I'll walk you to your car."

The rain had died down to a thin mist. A crescent moon peeked through small gaps in the fast-moving clouds. Somewhere, a cricket braved the cold weather to let out its reedy call.

"Your car doing all right?" asked Talli's father.

"Sure."

"And you're going to be okay?"

"Oh, Dad," Talli said. She grabbed the seam

33

of his coat and kissed him on the cheek. "I'll be fine. Go on to your conference. I'll take care of Mom."

The door of his old white pickup truck groaned as he pulled it open and threw his suitcase onto the bench seat. "I don't like leaving you alone. Especially after what happened today."

"Mom's here. She'll watch out for me."

"I thought you said you'd be taking care of her."

Talli shrugged. "I'll take care of her, and she'll take care of me."

"That's what I like to hear." He stepped up into the truck. "Be careful driving on these wet roads, all right?"

"Okay, Dad," Talli said. "You be careful too."

The big engine growled to life, and the truck bounced off into the gathering fog. Talli watched him go with a strange feeling of abandonment. Trying to shake off her gloom, she slid into the seat of her Pinto and headed back to the school. In the dark, she understood what Lisa had said about the town. With the leafless trees and shadowy buildings barely seen in the night, it did look spooky.

Without her father, Talli felt unprotected and lonely. As she drove into the dusk, she couldn't help feeling that something in the darkness was threatening her.

Four

The parking lot at school was more than large enough to hold the cars for a school-board meeting, and Talli was able to squeeze into a spot close to the door. She hurried in to find the board members already taking their seats around the long table at one end of the cafeteria.

Talli's chair was at the end of the table. In theory, as student representative, she was a member of the board. However, she was a non-voting member, and she couldn't remember the last time anyone on the board had asked for her opinion on anything. Even when students came to speak to the board, they never talked to Talli. It seemed to be expected that she would be seen and not heard.

The crowd for this meeting was smaller than usual. With the short notice, many of the people that usually came to meetings probably hadn't even heard about it. But there were some visitors in the seats. In the front row was Howard Lansky, one of Westerberg's six police officers. Beside him were Principal Volker and Assistant Principal Lynch. The massive muscles in Lynch's shoulders and arms seemed about to pop through the material of his suit.

The head of the school board, a large woman in a plaid suit, pounded an ashtray on the table to bring the meeting to order.

"I want to thank everyone for being here tonight," she said. "I'm afraid I had to call this meeting for an unpleasant reason. Our new principal, Mr. Volker, has had a busy first day on the job, and we have some decisions to make tonight that may affect the future of Westerberg High School for some time to come." She gestured to the principal with a pudgy hand. "Mr. Volker, would you please explain today's events?"

Volker rose from his seat and strode briskly to the front of the room. His gray hair glistened under the lights. His gray suit was immaculately pressed. "Gentlemen and ladies of the school board," he said in the same soft, clipped voice Talli had heard in the hallway behind the stage. "First I'd like to thank you for the confidence you showed in me by offering me this position. I know that the departure of Mr. Shay was quite a shock, and I'm only glad that I was available to fill in until you can find a proper replacement."

He put his long-fingered hands on the table, and his thin face grew solemn. "I'm sorry to report that this afternoon, an incident of a very serious nature occurred in Westerberg High. Two female students, fine, outstanding students, were threatened by two male students bearing knives."

There was mumbling from a few of the school-board members and the small audience. Volker raised one hand in a calming gesture.

"Fortunately, Mr. Lynch and myself were present to put an end to the incident. We took the individuals in hand and turned them over to the local police. A subsequent search revealed that one of the male students was carrying a gun, as well as a knife."

The mumbling from the school board grew in pitch. "Were the girls hurt?" asked a man at one end of the table.

A thin smile appeared on Volker's face. "I am happy to report that they were not. In fact, one of the young ladies involved was our own Ms. McAlister here." He gestured toward Talli, and she felt a blush spread up from her neck. "Are you all right, Ms. McAlister?"

"Yes," Talli said. She was embarrassed by how her throat had tightened under Volker's gaze, turning her answer into a squeak. She had never expected him to point her out in public.

The school-board president stepped in.

"What we have to decide," she said, "is how we're going to handle this."

"What's being done with the attackers?" someone asked.

Sergeant Howard Lansky stood. "I can answer that," he said. He pulled a pack of cigarettes from his pocket and tapped one out into his hand. "I've got the two perpetrators up at the station right now. They're being charged with assault and possession of a concealed weapon." He shoved the cigarette into his mouth and stuffed the pack back into his shirt pocket before sitting down. "I expect they won't be disturbing the other students for some time to come."

"How are we going to prevent something like this from happening again?" asked the president. She took a glossy folder from the table and passed it to the board member next to her. "I picked up these brochures on metal detectors," she continued. "Terrible as it sounds, I think we're going to have to install a system to prevent knives and guns from entering the school."

"No," said Volker. He reached out and plucked the brochure from the dangling fingers of the school-board member. "There's no need for anything like this. We can handle the situation without resorting to searching every student." He began to pace slowly down the length of the table.

"A lot of schools are installing detectors

these days," said the president. "We have to keep our students safe."

Volker stopped in front of her. "I'll take care of the students," he said. He placed his hands on the table and leaned toward her, staring into her eyes. "Give me a week. You will see what I'm capable of."

"It's a very dangerous . . ."

"One week," Volker said. "Just one week."

The woman hesitated, and Talli saw her mouth the words as Volker spoke.

"Well," she said woodenly. "I guess one week won't hurt."

"I'm not sure we can simply rely on trust," said another board member. "We should at least search the school. If we turn up more weapons, we should take measures immediately."

Volker turned away from the president and stepped over to the man who had spoken. Talli watched Volker's face as he closed on the man. There was a slight smile on the principal's thin lips, but his dark eyes were as cold as stone.

"No such measures are necessary," Volker said. "The two miscreants have been removed. I will take care of the situation. One week."

"One week," repeated the board member.

"That's right. One week and everything will be different."

"Are we all in agreement, then?" asked the board president. "Mr. Volker will handle this situation as he sees fit until our next meeting?"

There were general nods along the table. "All right, then. There are a few minor matters that we should—"

"Excuse me," Talli said. Every head in the room turned toward her.

"Was there something you wanted to say, Ms. McAlister?" Volker asked.

Talli nodded. She had to clear her throat before she could continue. "You said two male students. What about the third one?"

"Third one?" asked a school-board member. "Was there another student involved?"

"He didn't point a knife at us," Talli said, "but he was there. And what about the drugs he had with him?"

"Drugs?" asked the school-board president. "There were drugs involved in this?"

Volker walked over to Talli and looked down at her with an expression of concern. "I'm afraid I don't know what Ms. McAlister is talking about," he said.

"The guy in the prop room," Talli said. "The one that was sitting on the floor and laughing."

Volker shook his head. "Ms. McAlister, Tallibeth, you haven't been using drugs yourself, have you?"

Talli felt her face color again. Her ears felt as though they were burning. "I'm not taking drugs!" she choked out angrily.

Volker turned to the school-board president. "It was a very stressful day. I'm afraid that Ms.

McAlister isn't quite remembering things as they actually occurred."

The board president nodded. "Now, if we can get on to these other matters."

Talli started to protest, but Volker's eyes fastened on her. The weight of his stare seemed to sap the strength from Talli. She sagged in her chair, gasping for breath. Volker nodded slightly, then walked back to his seat in the front row of the audience.

Talli watched him for some time, but his attention was fixed on the school-board president, and his cold eyes didn't turn back to her. Still feeling confused and weakened, her gaze slipped over to Lynch.

The assistant principal's gray eyes were focused right on Talli. As she watched, a smile formed on his broad face. But it wasn't friendly.

It wasn't friendly at all.

41

Five

Wednesday

Talli pulled the old yearbook from the library shelf and carried it over to the table where Lisa was waiting. She dropped it with a thunk that might have gotten her a reprimand in more peaceful times. But since Westerberg had become so crowded, noise in the library was expected.

"You really think he's going to be in there?" Lisa asked.

"I don't remember him here before," Talli said. "Do you?"

"No."

"Then he must have come over from Cushing High." Talli opened the black and gold cover of the yearbook and turned to the first page. "What grade do you think he's in?"

"Who knows?" Lisa said. "And don't forget that he might have transferred in from someplace else. He might not even be a student at all."

"Thanks for the optimism," Talli said. "I think he looked like a senior, so he must have been a junior last year." She flipped quickly past the pages of freshmen and sophomores and focused on the first page of black and white pictures from Cushing High's last class of juniors.

Lisa peered over her shoulder. "It's hard to tell anything from these little pictures." She ran her finger down the page. "I still can't believe Volker said there were only two guys."

"Well, he did," Talli said. "I don't see him on this page. You?"

"Nope," Lisa said.

Talli flipped the page, and they scanned another hundred postage-stamp-size faces. Talli squinted at each one in turn, looking for the face of the guy who had sat on the prop-room floor while his friends threatened her and Lisa. Page after page went by, and while they saw many faces that looked familiar from the crowded halls of Westerberg, none of them resembled the blond guy they were looking for.

"I guess you were right," Talli said at last. "He's probably not even a student." She started to close the yearbook.

"Wait!" Lisa cried. She stopped Talli's hand

and forced the book open. "Look there." She was pointing at a group of pictures set off from the rest of the class, four larger portraits that showed the junior-class officers. Lisa stabbed her finger down on one of the pictures. "That's him."

Talli stared at the photograph. It was hard to imagine that this healthy-looking face belonged to the same guy that had sat on the floor and tittered like a hyena, but she thought Lisa was right. "He was president of his class last year!" Talli said in wonder. "He sure has changed."

"Morris South," Lisa said slowly. "He's actually good-looking in this picture."

"Well," Talli replied, "the important thing is that we found him. Now we have to figure out why Volker didn't punish him."

"Maybe he wasn't doing anything."

"Lisa! Come on. You saw him there with those drugs."

"We don't know that it was drugs in those bags," Lisa said.

Talli laughed. "Yeah, right. They were selling talcum powder. Besides, if he wasn't doing anything wrong, why didn't he help us?"

"I don't know. Maybe he was just scared."

"Well, why did Volker say he wasn't there at all?"

Lisa's mouth twisted in a puzzled frown. "I don't know. Maybe he was trying to protect him.

Maybe Morris is going to be a witness against some bigger bad guys."

"I don't think so," Talli said. "Volker had some reason for not bringing this guy in, and I'd like to know what it is."

"Volker saved our necks yesterday. Can't you give him a break?"

Before Talli could reply, a large hand swept down and pulled the yearbook from the table. Talli looked up to see Assistant Principal Lynch glaring down at them.

"I agree with your friend," he said in his reedy voice. "Mr. Volker has taken care of you, and you're not being very loyal."

"I have nothing against Volker," Talli said. "I just want to know what's going on."

Lynch leaned down until the ends of his long mustache almost brushed Talli's face. "I think your attitude needs improvement," he said. "You shouldn't be so disrespectful to Mr. Volker."

Talli swallowed hard and tried to match Lynch's glare with one of her own. "What were you doing?" she asked. "Spying on us? What we were talking about is none of your business."

"Everything in this school is my business," Lynch said. He straightened and tugged at the sleeves of his tight suit coat. "Don't forget that." With the Cushing High yearbook still in his hand, he turned and walked quickly out of the library.

"Well, wasn't that nice?" Lisa whispered.

"Still think he's kind of cute?" Talli asked.

Lisa shook her head. "What I think is that you had better watch it," she said, "or we'll both end up in big trouble."

The bell rang, signaling the end of the period and the end of the school day. Lisa stood up quickly and gathered her things.

"I'll call you tonight," Talli told her. "I want to talk some more about Volker."

Lisa wrinkled her nose and looked around. "All right, I guess. I don't suppose Lynch is tapping our phones."

"Not yet, anyway," Talli said. "I'm going to the library with Alex tonight. I'll call you after, okay?"

"Sure. Study hard." Lisa clutched her books to her chest and joined the crush of students heading for the front door.

Talli took her time getting ready to leave. She went over to the shelf, but she couldn't find another copy of the Cushing High yearbook. By the time she had picked up her things and left the library, the stream of students on their way out had become a trickle.

Outside, the rain had stopped, but it had turned colder. Talli zipped her jacket as she stepped out into a chilling wind and sloshed off across the still-wet parking lot. Without the rain, the town looked a little brighter, but Talli could think of nothing except Lynch's threatening words in the library and Volker's smooth lies at the meeting the previous night. As she drove past Volker's rented house, Talli slowed. Nothing could be seen through its long windows, but she felt colder just looking at the house.

Talli was barely through the door of her own house when her mother came down the stairs. "There you are," she said. "I just got off the phone with your principal."

Talli froze in the middle of taking her coat off. "Yeah? What did he want?"

Mrs. McAlister tilted her head. Her hair, shorter and not so red as Talli's, fell against the side of her face. "He just called to say how much he appreciated your work on the student council."

"That's . . . that's great," Talli said.

"It sure is. He could help you get into the college you want."

Talli took off her coat and started toward her room, but her mother stopped her with a gentle hand on her shoulder.

"Tallibeth," she said softly. "Is everything okay?"

Talli shrugged. She thought of telling her mother about Lynch, but she was afraid it would sound kind of lame. "Sure, everything's fine. Why wouldn't it be?"

"I don't know, but I worry about you. It's part of being a mother, I guess." She smiled. "As soon as you've put your things away, why don't you come down to the kitchen? We'll see what we can stuff in the microwave, and maybe you and I can eat dinner together for once."

"Sounds good," Talli said. She tried to return her mother's smile. "I'll be right down."

She hurried upstairs to her room and threw her books on the bed. There was a knot in her stomach, a tight ball of emotions she couldn't put a name to. She only knew that she didn't like Volker calling her at home.

She turned to the window. Over the roof of the house next door, she could see the upper story of Volker's house. Its windows were dark and empty. Talli couldn't remember if she had ever seen a light in those windows.

"Stay away from me," she whispered to the darkness that seemed to pour from the house. She turned her back on it and went downstairs.

Talli helped her mother lay out the food, and they dined on a smorgasbord of leftovers. While she was still eating, Talli saw a familiar car pull into the driveway. "Got to run," she said. "Alex is here."

"I was hoping you'd stay in tonight," Mrs. McAlister said. "You were out last night with the school board, and the night before that with Lisa."

"It's a study date, Mom. There's a big math test coming up."

"Just make sure there's more study than date," Mrs. McAlister replied.

48

"Okay," Talli said. She kissed her mother and ran for the door. As she climbed into the car, she was surprised to see Alex looking at her with a very serious expression on his face.

"Why didn't you tell me?" he asked.

"Tell you what?"

"You know."

"I don't know," Talli said. "What are you talking about?"

"Two guys pull knives on you at school, and you don't even tell me about it?" Alex asked.

Talli shrugged. "I didn't want to upset you, I guess. How did you hear about it, anyway?"

Alex's frown deepened. "Tom Rogers told me. His dad's on the school board." He reached out and took hold of Talli's arm. "How can I take care of you if you don't tell me what's going on?"

Now it was Talli's turn to frown. She pulled away from his grip. "Take care of me? You're not Tarzan, and I'm not Jane. I take care of myself."

"I don't mean . . ." Alex started. "Damn. I don't know *what* I mean. I just don't want to see you get hurt."

"That makes two of us," Talli said. She reached over, took his hand, and squeezed it. "Don't worry. I really can take care of myself."

Alex nodded, and the tension in his face drained away. "I hear the new principal came through like a marine," he said.

"Yeah. Volker was great. Can we get going?"

"Sure." Alex popped the car into gear and

they sped off up the dark road. "So are we actually going to study?"

Talli nodded. "Oh, absolutely. There's a math test coming up, you know."

"Yeah, I know. But we already spent a whole night on that. How much longer do you figure we have to study?"

"Let me see." Talli pursed her lips and made a show of counting on her fingers. "I figure twenty minutes for studying, and two hours for seeing *Daughter of Blood* at the movies!"

Alex shook his head. "You're an evil person, you know that? Don't you ever get enough of those horror movies?"

"No," Talli said. "So hurry up and drive or we'll miss the seven o'clock show."

Westerberg's theater had been out of business for twenty years, but there was one a few miles down the road in Crickton. Talli and Alex made it to the ticket window with five minutes to spare. Alex bought snacks from the refreshment stand while Talli bought the drinks, and they were ready for two hours of popcorn and B-movie mayhem.

Talli had loved horror films ever since she was little. The old black-and-white movies from the thirties and forties had captured her imagination from the time she was old enough to watch. At an age when most kids were frozen in front of cartoons, Talli was watching *Frankenstein*, *The Wolfman*, and *Dracula*. And then there were horror books. From the fairy-tale witch to the latest slasher novel, Talli read them all and loved every scary page.

For ninety minutes, she leaned against Alex and watched the fake blood flow across the screen. Sometimes, if the movie was very good, the screen would disappear. Then, for a few moments, Talli would be *in* the picture, a part of the action. *Daughter of Blood* was not that good.

"Kind of disappointing," Alex said as they walked out of the theater and climbed into his car.

"I don't know," Talli said. "There were a few good scenes."

"Is that what you're going to do when you get out of school?" Alex asked as they drove from the parking lot.

"What?"

"Make horror movies."

Talli shrugged. "I don't know. I think maybe I'd like to write."

"You could start by showing me some of those stories you've written," suggested Alex.

"No way. No one sees my stories."

"Hard to have a career if you don't have any fans."

"I'll worry about fans later. Right now I'm still learning to put words on paper."

"So, where are we going to study?"

"I'm kind of hungry," Talli said. "How about you?"

"I'm always hungry."

"All right, then, let's go back to Westerberg and find someplace to eat."

"Deal," Alex said.

Eight thirty was late enough for almost everything in Crickton and Westerberg to be closed. With all the windows black and the signs turned off, it looked like a ghost town as they drove through downtown. Only on the outskirts of town, where the new fast-food places clustered together at the edge of the darkness, was there any sign of life.

Talli couldn't shake off the jumpy mood of the movie. Westerberg seemed as spooky as any horror movie she had ever seen. She huddled in her seat as they drove past the school. Glancing over at it, Talli stiffened, alarm ringing in every nerve.

"Alex," she said fearfully, "what's that?"

Six

꙳꙳꙳

Alex turned to look across the road. "It's school, of course."

"Not the school, the parking lot. See that car by the door?"

"Yeah."

"It's Volker's car," Talli said. "I've seen it at his house."

Alex shrugged. "Principal's car found in school parking lot," he said. "Is this a big mystery?"

"It is when it's this late. Turn up there, into the park."

"Why?"

"So we can watch him."

"What?"

"Just do it," Talli said. "Pull up there by the water tower. Then we can see down, but he'll have a hard time seeing us."

Alex shook his head, but he followed Talli's instructions. "Now what?"

"Now turn off the car and kill the lights."

"This is crazy," he said. "Why are we spying on the principal?"

"Because there's something fishy about him," Talli said.

"Does this have anything to do with what happened to you at school?" Alex asked.

"Kind of. Volker told the school board that there were two guys in the prop room."

"So?"

"There were three guys."

"Maybe he made a mistake."

"Nope," Talli said. "When I reminded him, he said the other guy never existed. And they had drugs. Volker never said a thing about that—except when he asked if *I* was using drugs!"

"He said that?"

"Yeah, right in front of the school board." Talli leaned forward and rested her chin on the cool vinyl of the dashboard. "Everyone thinks Mr. Principal Volker is such a hero, but there's something really strange about him."

Alex slid his arm around her shoulders. "Why aren't you telling me these things?" he asked. "First the guys that attacked you, now this stuff with Volker."

"It only happened yesterday," Talli said. "There hasn't been time."

"It still seems like . . ." Alex started.

Talli frowned. "Like what?"

"Sorry, I was watching the school," he said. "They turned the lights on."

Talli turned and saw that the windows of the school, which had been dark, were glowing with light. It spilled out onto the parking lot and cast a long shadow from Volker's parked car.

"Those aren't the regular lights," Talli said.

"What?"

"Look at the color," she said. "Those aren't the regular lights." The fluorescent tubes that lined Westerberg High's hallways produced a light that was very steady and white. The light coming from the school now pulsed and flickered like the glow from a bonfire, and it wasn't white—it was the yellow-green color of lightning bugs dying in a jar. It made Talli think of some phosphorescent plant that lived in a dank swamp, or of glowing fish in the deep ocean, where light never came.

"Of course it's the lights," Alex said. "What else could it be?"

Talli shook her head. "I don't know, but that's *not* coming from any light bulb."

"Maybe it's the emergency lighting."

"I don't think so."

"Come on, Talli," Alex said. There was a hint of irritation creeping into his voice. "I think we've gone to too many horror movies."

As suddenly as it had begun, the verdant

55

light flickered and faded. For a moment it flared again, so brightly that even the trees on the edge of the parking lot cast sharp shadows on the soggy ground. Then it was gone.

"Still think it's the regular lights?" Talli said.

"I think we should get going," Alex said. "We still have studying to do."

He put his hand on the gearshift, but Talli put her hand over his. "Let's go down there," she whispered.

"No way!" Alex said.

Talli smiled at him and raised one eyebrow. "Why?" she asked. "You afraid?"

"Yes," said Alex.

"Then you admit that there's something strange going on with Volker?"

"There's something going on," he replied. "But what I'm afraid of is getting in trouble for snooping around at night. I sure don't think there are any bogeymen down there."

"You saw that light."

"Yeah, but for all you know, they could be welding pipes in the hallway. It doesn't have to be anything weird."

Talli opened her mouth to object, then closed it again. "You're right," she said after a moment. "The lights don't really mean anything." She bit her lip, remembering how peculiar she had felt when Volker took her hand, and when he had stared at her at the board meeting. How could she explain those things to Alex?

56

"I still think something strange is going on," she said.

"Let's go find something to eat," Alex suggested. "I've heard that talking about ghosts and goblins on an empty stomach causes ulcers."

Talli punched him on the arm, but his humor made her feel better. "There could be Martians taking over our school, and you can't think of anything but your stomach."

"At least I have my priorities right," he said. "Can we go?"

"I guess so," Talli said.

The words were barely out of her mouth when the door opened and three figures walked out of the school. Both Alex and Talli froze as the forms crossed the short gap of dark sidewalk and climbed into Volker's car.

"The tall one has to be Volker," Talli said.

"And the gorilla is Lynch," Alex said. "But who's the other guy?"

Talli peered into the blackness as the third man opened his door and slid in. "I can't tell," she said. "It's too dark."

Volker's car pulled out of the parking lot and turned down the road to the park. Talli instinctively ducked as the car swept past their hiding place. With her eyes barely peeking over the dashboard, she caught a glimpse of Lynch's face behind the wheel. In the seat next to him was a thin young man with yellow hair.

"Morris South!" she whispered.

"Who?" Alex said. Like Talli, he had ducked as the principal's car passed.

Talli sat up and watched the taillights disappear around a turn in the road. "The guy I was telling you about," she said. "The one that was there when those dopers pulled knives on me and Lisa. The one Volker covered up for."

"You sure it was him?"

"Positive."

"I wonder what he was doing in Volker's car?" Alex asked.

"Now do you believe me?" Talli asked. "There *is* something weird going on around here."

"Yeah," he replied, "and I think I know what it is. Are you sure those guys had drugs?"

"Definitely. Baggies of something."

"But Volker didn't mention the drugs when he was talking to the school board?"

"No," Talli said, "and the police don't know about them, either."

Alex held up a finger. "One: there are drug pushers in the school." He flipped up another finger. "Two: Volker just happens to be there when you run into them. Three: Volker covers up for one of the guys. Four: Volker never says anything about the drugs. Five: Volker is hanging around the school at night with one of the druggies."

"You think he's part of it?" Talli asked.

Alex nodded. "I think super-principal is selling drugs to the kids."

Talli settled back in her seat and stared out at the dark school. "So what do we do about it?" she asked. "Go to the police?"

"I'm not sure we can," Alex said. "We don't have any real evidence. It's your word against his."

"Dad and the sheriff are both out of town," Talli said. "That leaves Sergeant Lansky in charge." She shook her head. "He's already on Volker's side."

"You don't think he's in on this too, do you?"

"No," she said, "but he seemed pretty friendly with Volker at the meeting."

"So let's wait till your dad gets back," Alex said. "Then we can talk to him about it."

"Can we wait that long? He'll be gone until Saturday."

Alex gave her a comforting squeeze. "Sure. We'll stay out of Volker's way for the rest of the week. When your dad gets back, we'll tell him what we know."

Talli bit her lip and nodded slowly. "You're right," she said. "Dad will know how to take care of this."

"Now let's go get that food!"

They feasted on burgers, and talked about anything but Volker and his strange friends. Only when Alex was taking Talli back to her house, and they passed the dark silent bulk of Volker's residence, did the conversation turn back to what they had seen.

"What about that light?" Talli asked, looking over the high fence that surrounded Volker's house. As usual, the empty windows of the second story were black. "How does that fit in?"

"I don't know," Alex said, "but your dad will find out."

"I guess so," Talli said. Volker's house dropped out of sight as they turned into her driveway.

Alex stopped the car behind Talli's house. "So," he said, "how long do you think we have until your mom looks out to see what we're doing in the car?"

"About ten minutes," Talli said.

"Then let's use them." He reached over and pulled her to him.

Talli smiled as she put her hands behind his head and pulled his lips down to hers. But even in the middle of a kiss, she could not stop feeling that something was very, very wrong.

And it was going to get worse.

Seven

Thursday

The paint on Talli's locker had dried and faded to a dark red smear. She tried to avoid the stain as she shut the door and headed off for her first class of the day. She was almost through the classroom door when she heard a familiar voice calling her name. She looked up to see Samantha Deveraux cutting through the hallway toward her.

The crowd seemed to part before Samantha's short red dress. "I've been looking for you everywhere," Samantha declared as she approached.

Talli considered ducking into her classroom, but there was no getting around talking to Samantha eventually. "You seem to have a lot of trouble with that," Talli said. "I'm in the same place every day."

Samantha seemed to consider that remark for a moment, then she gave Talli a smile filled with lip gloss and cosmetically whitened teeth. "So, tell me about the meeting," she said.

"Meeting?"

"The school-board meeting," Samantha said. "I heard that something interesting happened."

Talli fought back the urge to tell her to attend her own meetings if she wanted the news. But arguing with Samantha never accomplished anything. "Some students got in trouble for bringing knives into the school. The board wanted to put in metal detectors and stuff. Principal Volker talked them out of it."

"Oh," Samantha said. "Is that all?"

The bell rang to signal the start of class, and Talli tried to edge away from Samantha. "That's all. I've got to—"

"There's one other thing."

"What?"

"The Read-A-Thon fund-raiser."

"What about it?" Talli asked.

"It's starting next week," Samantha said. "The school board has always handled it. I thought that since you were always, you know, reading . . ." She stopped to wrinkle her small upturned nose. "I thought you should handle it."

"Sam, I'm already doing the board meetings and writing everything up for the school paper. Don't you think you could handle this one by yourself?"

Samantha looked around as if she had just noticed the empty hall. "Uh-oh. Class is starting. Let's get together and talk about it after school. Okay?"

"Sam, I—"

"By the front door, all right?"

"Sam—"

"I'll see you there." Samantha brushed past Talli and sauntered up the hall with her high heels tapping a staccato rhythm against the tiles.

Talli turned and went into class. She dropped into a chair behind Lisa, who turned and said, "Oh, Talli, would you please be my slave and do all my work for me?"

Talli mimed a scream.

The teacher rapped a pointer against the board, and the conversations in the room died from a roar to a rumble. "Before we get started today," announced the teacher, "I want to relay a new policy from the office. Principal Volker is very interested in discipline. Therefore, we have been instructed to send every discipline problem to him on the first offense."

"Never happen," whispered Lisa. "Principals always say that crap, but they really don't want all the hassle."

"Ms. Taylor," said the teacher. "Would you like to be the first to experience this new system?"

"No, sir," Lisa said.

The teacher turned to the chalkboard and started his lecture. Whether it was fear of the new rules or not, he got through almost ten minutes of the lesson before there was any major interruption. By Talli's estimate that was a new record for Westerberg in this year of anarchy.

Then a weasely kid named Paul Katz got sent to the office for mouthing off to the teacher. Five minutes later Cheryl Fellini joined him when her whispered conversation with a friend turned into an argument.

Talli saw them leave with an odd feeling of apprehension, but they were both back within ten minutes. She watched them closely after their return. Paul seemed very subdued. In fact, Talli thought he was going to fall asleep at his desk. Cheryl seemed none the worse for the visit to Volker's office. With the first two violators back without scars, the class opened up a bit, and three or four more students were soon on their way out the door. Still, the hassle of having to walk down to the office was enough to cut the problems in the class by at least fifty percent.

When the bell rang, Talli whispered quickly to Lisa, "You talk to Paul Katz. I'm going to talk to Cheryl."

"Why do I want to talk to Katz the Rat?" Lisa asked.

"To find out what Volker did to him."

"You're still after Volker and his charming assistant, Mr. Orangutan?"

"Just talk to Paul before he gets away," Talli said. "I'll explain later."

Talli caught Cheryl Fellini at the door. "What did he do to you?" she asked.

"What?"

"Volker. What did he do when you went to his office?"

"Oh," Cheryl said. "He gave me detention. Can you believe it? Two days of after-school detention, just for talking in class."

Lisa came strolling up as Cheryl walked out into the hall. "The Rat got detention for the rest of the week," she said.

"So did Cheryl," Talli said.

"Yeah, well, I hope you're satisfied," Lisa said. "I'm probably the only girl to talk to the Rat in a month." She shivered dramatically. "He probably thinks I like him."

Talli looked around to make sure that no one else was around before speaking. "Last night Alex and I drove past the school."

"And?"

"And we saw Volker here in the middle of the night—with Morris South."

Lisa's brown eyes opened wide. "The guy we found in that yearbook?"

Talli nodded. "The guy that had the drugs when those jerks pulled knives on us."

Lisa stepped closer and spoke in an excited whisper. "All right, Volker is definitely up to something. And it's getting weird. Any ideas?"

"Alex thinks he's involved in getting drugs into the school. We're going to talk to my dad when he gets back."

The second bell sounded. "Got to go," Lisa said. "I'm supposed to be all the way on the other side of the building in two minutes. See you in history." She ran for the hallway.

Talli's class was closer, but she still barely made it. Volker's new rule about being sent to the office was repeated by the teacher. The word about what happened when you went there must have gotten around, because only one student got sent to visit Volker. Everybody hated after-school detention. It was about the worst thing a teacher could do to you. Usually it didn't come up much, because it made the teachers have to stay after too, and they didn't like it any better than the students. Volker seemed prepared to stay late every day.

Talli continued to observe the students that came back from Volker's office. Most of them looked okay, but a couple seemed to be exhausted. In third period one girl came back acting worse than before. She was so hyper that the teacher soon sent her to see Volker a second time. She didn't make it back before the end of class.

When Talli had class with Lisa again after lunch, they compared notes. "Not too many people got sent," Lisa reported. "I think this is probably the calmest day of the year."

"Yeah, Volker's method seems to be working. You notice anything about the people that got sent?"

"Like what?"

"Like, did any of them fall asleep?"

Lisa shook her head. "Not that I noticed. I wasn't really watching them, though."

They settled into chairs and opened their notebooks. About halfway through the class, there was a burst of laughter from the back of the room. Talli turned in time to see Ashley Westin swat at the guy next to her.

"Ashley," said the teacher, Ms. Batkawitz. "Do you want to leave this class?"

"You didn't hear what he said!" Ashley replied.

"No, but I saw what you did."

Ashley scowled, but settled back in her chair and looked down at her papers. Talli turned around, but Ms. Batkawitz had barely gotten out another sentence before there was a loud smack from the back of the room, followed by a crash. When Talli looked back, Ashley was on her feet beside an overturned desk. Her purse and books were spread across the classroom floor, and she was glaring at the guy she had slapped a moment before. "Make him stop!" she shouted.

"Both of you go to the office," Ms. Batkawitz said.

"But I didn't do anything!" protested the guy.

"Tell it to Mr. Volker. Now go!"

Still steaming, Ashley stamped out of the room. The guy she had been fighting with—a tall, brown-haired guy whose name Talli had never learned—slowly got out of his chair and followed her. There was a satisfied smirk on his face.

Ten minutes later, Talli was so intent on her notes that she didn't notice Ashley's return to the room until she bumped into Talli's desk. Talli looked up to see Ashley stagger away from the impact and drop into her chair like a sack of potatoes.

"Are you going to cause more problems, Ashley?" Ms. Batkawitz asked.

Ashley shook her head. She looked as green as the paint on the walls.

"Are you okay?" Talli asked.

"Talli," Ms. Batkawitz said. "Please don't encourage her."

"She looks sick," Talli said.

"Are you all right, Ashley?" asked the teacher.

Ashley opened her mouth, but no words came out. She nodded her head. Her hands shook as she reached down to pick up one of her books.

"Ashley?"

The girl nodded again and opened her textbook. Ms. Batkawitz looked concerned, but after a moment she turned back to the board and continued her lecture.

Suddenly there was another crash from the back of the room. Talli turned to see that Ashley's desk was again on its side, and Ashley stood beside it.

Ms. Batkawitz sighed. "All right," she said tiredly. "Who did it this time?"

Ashley screamed.

Eight

❦

It wasn't a pretty scream—not the kind reserved for a horror movie, or the tallest hill on the roller coaster—it was a long, painful scream. The sound made the hair on Talli's neck stand up and raised goose bumps on her arms. Half the kids in the classroom screamed in reply.

Ashley suddenly leaped forward and stood swaying in the aisle between desks. Her head rolled around as if her neck were broken. She stretched her arms up to the sky, her fingers twisted like claws. She raised one foot from the floor, and for a crazy moment, Talli thought she was going to dance. Then Ashley fell into a heap on the floor.

There was a second in which everything seemed terribly still. No one moved. No one talked. Then everyone was running and talking and screaming all at once. Ashley began to jerk and twitch, kicking desks and pounding her hands against the linoleum tiles.

Ms. Batkawitz came around her desk, running toward the fallen girl. She grabbed a student out of the front row and shoved him toward the door. "Get the nurse! Fast! And tell her to call an ambulance!"

A half-dozen students ran out the door, some of them still screaming as they went. Others had pressed themselves against the wall, staying as far away from the fallen Ashley as they could.

On the tiled floor, Ashley continued to jerk and thrash. Her arms and legs struck the metal legs of desks, toppling more seats and sending loose papers and books flying.

Talli tried to grab one flailing arm, but it was like grabbing a machine. Ashley seemed to have the strength of a gorilla, and Talli was knocked away.

Ms. Batkawitz came up behind Ashley's lolling head and pulled it onto her lap. One of Ashley's arms came up and struck her against the cheek, but the teacher hung on. "Everyone stay back!" she called.

"What's wrong with her?" Talli asked.

"It's some kind of seizure." Another blow glanced off the teacher's face, sending her glasses flying across the room. Ms. Batkawitz winced. "Ashley? Can you hear me? Calm down, Ashley! We're trying to take care of you."

71

Talli couldn't tell if any of the teacher's words were getting through. Ashley kept on twisting. One of her feet caught in the base of a desk, and there was a squeal as the metal legs of the desk were dragged across the tile floor.

"Should we do something?" Lisa asked.

"Will she swallow her tongue?" asked another student.

"I don't know," Ms. Batkawitz said. Sprawled on the floor and without her glasses, the teacher looked almost as young and scared as her students. "We just have to wait for the nurse."

Ashley's eyes rolled up, leaving only a wide space of white. Foam dripped from the side of her mouth. The beating of her heels against the floor was loud and fast. In the back of the room, someone started to cry.

Lisa slid around to stand next to Talli. "This is scary," she whispered. "You think she has something that's catching?"

"I don't think so," Talli said.

The nurse charged into the room a second later. She glanced at the scene on the floor and went to sit beside the teacher. "An ambulance is on the way," she said.

"Thank God," Ms. Batkawitz said.

"What happened here?"

"I don't know. She fell down and started shaking."

"Did she hit her head?" asked the nurse.

"I think so," the teacher replied, "but the shaking started before that."

Ashley groaned, and her eyelids closed over her empty eyes. Her legs stopped their wild dance, and her arms stopped pounding everything in reach.

"It looks like the worst is over," said the nurse.

Ms. Batkawitz nodded. "I didn't know what to do," she said.

"You did fine."

Ashley grunted, and a thin stream of blood trickled from the corner of her mouth. The nurse grabbed her chin and pulled her mouth open. "She's bitten her tongue! We need to get something in her mouth so it won't happen again."

"A pencil?" suggested one student.

"Breaks too easily," said the nurse.

"How about this?" suggested a thin boy. He pulled a heavy metal ruler from his folder and passed it over.

"Perfect," said the nurse. She pulled Ashley's mouth open and pushed the ruler between her teeth.

"Saved by the nerd," Lisa whispered in Talli's ear.

It took another five minutes for the paramedics to arrive. They were still in the process of getting Ashley loaded onto a stretcher when the bell rang. Talli left the class reluctantly. Out in the hall, she pulled Lisa aside, trying to avoid the crush of passing students.

"What do you think?" she asked.

"About what?" Lisa said.

"About Ashley."

Lisa's brow creased. "I don't know. You think you know what's wrong with her?"

Talli nodded. "I think it's Volker."

"Volker?" Lisa asked. "How could he have anything to do with this?"

"Remember me saying that Alex thinks Volker is involved with drugs?"

"Yeah."

"I think he's been giving drugs to the kids that get sent to detention."

Lisa eyes widened. "No way! Talli, I agree the guy is weird, but he couldn't get away with a thing like that."

"Think about it," Talli said. "He pulls out more students than any principal you ever heard of. They come back either zoned out or hyper. Then Ashley comes back and has a fit."

"No." Lisa shook her head. "*You* think about it. The first person back in class would be talking about it. They'd have the cops down on him in ten seconds flat."

Talli frowned. "That's true. But maybe he's doing something sneaky."

"Like what?"

"I don't know." Talli waved her free hand. "Maybe he's putting something in a soda and giving it to them, or a cookie."

"Hey," Lisa said. "If they were giving out free soda and cookies at the principal's office, you would definitely have heard about it. People would be lining up to go."

"Maybe he's putting it in the air."

"Talli, even if he could be giving people drugs, *why*? What's the point in drugging people like that?"

"He's trying to get them addicted," Talli said. "If he gets them hooked, they'll be better customers for his dealers."

"Oh, yeah. Ashley looked like she was *really* enjoying her experience." Lisa shook her head firmly. "It doesn't make any sense. If you try to tell anyone else a story like this, you're going to end up in the loony bin."

Talli thought for a moment. "I know how we can find out what's going on."

"How?"

"Volker's giving lots of people after-school detention, right?"

"Right."

"So," Talli said. "Volker has to stay with them after school. And while Volker is here, his house will be empty. So how about—"

"Uh-uh!" Lisa interjected. "No way. No how."

"You didn't even let me finish," Talli said.

"If you're going to suggest that we break into the principal's house, I don't want you to finish," Lisa replied.

"But then we would know for sure."

"What's wrong with the original plan? Why not wait for your dad to get back and talk to him?"

Talli bit her lip. "I don't know. It seems like a long time to let Volker get away with what I think he's doing."

Lisa put a gentle hand on her arm. "Try to wait. You saw what Volker did to those two jerks who were after us. Do you really want him mad at you?"

"I guess not," Talli said. She tried out a small grin. "You sure you won't help me break into Volker's house?"

"Positive."

"Even if we could find the school records and change your chemistry grade to an A?"

"Ha! It would take more than a little covert action to do that," Lisa said. She looked at Talli with mock severity. "Promise me you'll be good."

"I'll be careful."

"That's *not* the same thing."

"I know. But it's the best I can do."

Lisa frowned. "Then I guess I'll settle for that. You giving me a ride home today?"

"Yup," Talli said. "See you out front, after school. I'm supposed to talk to Samantha about some council thing."

Lisa rolled her eyes. "We might as well have detention," she said. "See you there."

*　　*　　*

During the afternoon classes, few students were sent to Volker. Those that went seemed fine when they came back. Talli tried to relax. Lisa was right; there was no way that Volker could be handing out drugs in his office. It was a stupid idea.

When the final bell rang, Talli made her way to the front door and found Lisa waiting. "No sign of the councilwoman in charge of hairstyling," Lisa said. "Do we really have to wait for her?"

Talli sighed. "I guess so. It's something to do with a fund-raiser."

Students streamed past for the first few minutes, heading for buses or for their cars. By fifteen minutes after the last bell, there was only a handful of students still waiting.

"You sure she's coming?"

"She told me to meet her here," Talli said.

"Is it possible that a brain like Samantha could forget something?" The sarcasm in Lisa's voice was as thick as cement.

Talli looked at her watch. "We'll give her five more minutes, okay?"

Lights began to click off in the halls of Westerberg High, as automatic timers darkened the halls and classrooms. A cluster of students went past clutching band instruments, then Talli and Lisa were alone in the lobby of the school. Far down a hallway, Talli could see a dark form moving from room to room. From the width of the shoulders, there was no doubt that it was Assistant Principal Lynch. He reached the other end of the hall and turned back toward the entrance.

"She's not coming," Lisa said.

"I guess you're right. Let's go."

Lisa pushed the door open, and Talli followed her out into the slanting afternoon light. As the door closed, Talli turned and glanced back into the school.

The light spilled down the hall and touched the hulking figure of Lynch. It fell across his thick legs and chest, leaving his head in shadow.

But it wasn't his impressive build that caught Talli's attention. It was his eyes. Even though his face was nothing more than a dark shadow, she could see his eyes clearly. They were glowing as scarlet as a pair of hot coals.

Nine

❧

"I should be back by eight," Mrs. McAlister said. "Do you want to come with me to the PTO meeting?"

"I don't think so," Talli said. "I had to spend half of Tuesday night there. I'll stay here and study."

Her mother smiled. "All right. You sure you'll be okay?"

"Why shouldn't I be?"

"I don't know. You've seemed nervous the last few days." Mrs. McAlister reached across the table and put her hand over Talli's. "Is something bothering you?"

Talli thought of telling her mother everything. But what would she say? Weird feelings. Funny looks. It wasn't exactly the kind of thing that was easy to explain.

79

"No, Mom," she said at last. "I'm all right."

"Everything going okay with Alex?"

"Sure, we're fine."

"And nothing wrong at school?"

Talli laughed. "Really, Mom. There's nothing wrong. Go to your meeting, all right?"

"I'm going," Mrs. McAlister replied. "But how about we have a talk when we get back?"

Talli nodded. "Sounds good."

As soon as her mother left for the meeting, Talli grabbed her books and carried them into the living room. She flipped on the television and sat on the couch with her legs crossed, glancing at the notes she had taken in each class. She tried to settle down and concentrate, but she felt restless.

After a few minutes, she got up and went upstairs. From the window of her room, she looked across at the empty windows of Volker's house. There wasn't much to see. No curtains or furniture. Nothing to give any hint about the man who suddenly had so much power at Westerberg High.

"Unless the emptiness says something," Talli whispered.

The sun had dipped below the horizon, and it was rapidly growing dark. All over the neighborhood, other houses were switching on their lights, but Volker's house sat like a block of shadow between all the pools of light.

Talli pressed her lips together tightly. With a

sense of determination, she turned away from the window. She went to the hall closet and pulled out a flashlight. From the coat rack, she selected a black hooded jacket. She pulled it on and checked herself in the mirror.

The jacket covered her arms, and the hood took care of her red hair. Her jeans were fairly new, and dark enough. The only spots that stood out were her hands and the pale oval of her face. Her green eyes looked very wide and frightened. She frowned at the image in the mirror.

"Stay calm," she told herself.

The phone rang, and Talli jumped as if she'd been stung. It rang twice more before she got her breathing under enough control to answer it. "Hello?"

"Hi, Talli. What are you doing tonight?"

"Alex," Talli said with relief. "Can you come over?"

"I guess," Alex said. "When do you want me?"

"Right now."

"Is it an emergency?"

"Sort of. Get here as fast as you can." Talli said good-bye and hung up the phone. She glanced again at her reflection in the mirror and had to smile. Talli McAlister, fearless investigator. She waited at the back door for Alex. As soon as his dark blue Mustang pulled into the driveway, she ran out to meet him. The air was cold against her face, filled with the biting smell of wood smoke from one of the neighbors' chimneys. Under the trees by the driveway, it was very dark.

"Are you okay?" Alex asked as he climbed out of the car.

"I'm fine," Talli said. "But I need your help."

"You had me worried," he said. "What's up?"

Talli took a deep breath. "I'm going over to Volker's house to see if I can find anything, and I want you to come with me." She said it very quickly, watching Alex's face for his reaction.

For a long moment, he said nothing. Then his face brightened in a mischievous smile. "Is that why you're dressed like somebody off an old *Mission: Impossible* show?"

"Will you go with me?" Talli asked again.

Alex shrugged. "I'd rather talk you out of it."

"I'm going."

"There is a little thing called the law. Being a policeman's daughter, I thought you might have heard of it."

"I'm going anyway," Talli said.

"That's what I figured." Alex shoved his hands into his coat pockets. "Yeah, I'll go with you," he said. "Who knows what you might get into if I don't?"

"Thanks," Talli said.

"So, do you have a plan for this secret mission?"

"We'll go along the fence next door." Talli flipped on the flashlight and waved it toward

Volker's house. "There's a fence around Volker's yard, but there's a loose board in the back."

"How do you know? Have you done this before?"

"The Decarlos used to live there," Talli said. "I used to sneak in to use their pool when they were away."

"So breaking and entering is not a new career for you," Alex said.

"Oh, shut up and follow me." Talli aimed the flashlight at the ground and walked under the maples beside the drive. She led Alex through the narrow strip of grass that separated her house from the house next door. From there, they slipped into a thin, weedy space that was walled in by a fence on one side and a thick hedge on the other. Alex had to turn sideways to fit through.

The fence at the neighbor's house was only chest high, and its loose wooden slats allowed a clear view of their backyard. When they reached Volker's house, the situation was very different. There the fence was almost ten feet high, and the rough, staggered boards blocked all sight of the lower level of the house and its grounds.

"The loose board is right around here," Talli said.

"Unless he's fixed it," Alex said.

But a few seconds later, Talli pushed on a board that swung in and away, leaving a dark gap in the fence. "This is it," she whispered. She stood for a moment, looking up at the house. Seen without the fence, it was easier to appreciate how big it was—easily twice the size of any other house in the neighborhood. But the ground floor didn't reveal anything that the upper floors hadn't—just more dark empty windows.

"Better turn off your flashlight," Alex whispered. "If anyone's here, they'll see that for sure."

Talli slid the switch, and the darkness closed in around them. It took several seconds for her eyes to adjust enough to see anything at all. She pushed her way through the gap in the boards, the rough wood scraping against her jacket as she passed.

"Wait up," whispered Alex. "I'm stuck."

Talli turned to see Alex's head sticking through the gap in the fence, along with one arm and shoulder. She took his waving hand and pulled. He came through, but it was a tight fit.

"That hurt!" Alex said.

"Shh. Come on, let's look at the house."

They crept across the open backyard. "Watch out for the dark spot," Talli said.

"What dark spot?" Alex asked.

Talli grabbed his arm. "The one right in front of your feet." She nodded toward the ground. "That's the cover of the pool. You step on that, you could end up making a dry dive into concrete."

"Gotcha, boss," he replied. "This is a big place." He looked up the steps that led to the screen door on the porch. "Looks like a nice place to live."

"Yeah, if you can afford it. Let's see if the porch is open." Talli stepped slowly up the concrete steps.

"Nope."

"What do you mean, nope?"

"I mean, I'm not going in," Alex said.

"We didn't come over here for nothing," protested Talli.

"We came over here to look," he replied. "We can look without going in. Right now, we can say we chased your cat over here, or something. We get caught inside, and we're history."

Talli searched for a comeback, but found none. "Okay. Let's take a look in some of these windows."

She came back down the steps, and they walked around to the side of the house. The sound of a car came from the street, and for a moment they both froze. Then the headlights flicked across the house, and the noise died as the car went past. Talli stuck her nose close to a dusty ground-floor window.

"I don't see anything," she said.

"Me neither."

"I'm trying the flashlight." Before Alex had

time to argue, Talli switched the light on and played it through the window.

"What do you know," Alex said. "Empty window, empty room."

The yellow light of the flashlight showed only dusty floorboards, and walls covered with pale paint. There was a small cardboard box in one corner of the room, but no furniture at all.

"Looks like the movers haven't come yet," Alex said.

Talli shook her head. "He's been here over a month. How long can it take?" She moved the light around, trying to find anything of interest, but there was only bare wood and dust. "Let's try the front window," she suggested.

"Someone might see us there."

"We'll just take a quick look," she said. "Come on."

Another car went past as they reached the corner of the house. Talli crouched down behind the square bulk of an air conditioner. Alex huddled beside her. Through the cold damp air, she could feel his comforting warmth. He put his hand on her shoulder, and she reached up to link her fingers with his. When the car passed, Talli stood and walked quickly around to the front of the house.

The metal gate at the driveway would make it easy for anyone passing along the street to see this part of the property. Talli hurried up the steps to the front of the house and beamed the light through the narrow window beside the door.

Alex trotted up beside her and looked over her shoulder. "What's that on the floor?" he asked.

"I don't know." Talli aimed the light down for a better look. "It's junk mail and stuff. There's a lot of it. That's weird," she said. "I wonder why Volker doesn't pick it up."

"Maybe he's a slob," Alex said. "If there was a law against that, I know a lot of people who would be behind bars." He leaned over her and pressed his face close to the glass. "See anything else in there?"

Talli scanned back and forth with the light. "There's another box over by the bottom of the stairs," she said. "That's the only thing I see. No furniture at all."

There was the distant sound of an engine as another car turned onto the street. "Come on," Alex said. "Let's get out of here before somebody sees us."

"Just a second." Talli moved to the window on the other side of the door and spotlighted the staircase. From where she stood, she could see the top, but couldn't see into any of the rooms on the second floor.

Headlights suddenly spilled over the front of the house. Talli turned, blinking at the lights as the car approached the iron gate. There was a click, then the hum of an electric motor, and the gate began to inch slowly open.

"Run!" Alex cried. He dashed down the steps and disappeared around the corner of the house.

For one awful moment, Talli couldn't move. The headlights of the car pinned her to the porch as firmly as nails. The car revved its engine as the gate opened completely. It rolled through onto the short stretch of drive that separated the house from the road.

Then the spell was broken. Talli ran down the steps two at a time. She hadn't turned out the flashlight, and the beam swung wildly as she ran, picking out images in flashes: the dark brown trunk of an ancient apple tree, a patch of slippery grass, the pale boards along the side of the house.

Talli dodged around the air conditioner she had hidden behind before. As she approached the rear corner of the house, Talli ran headlong into something that grunted and staggered. She fell back and began to scream.

"Talli! It's me," said the dark form.

Talli brought the flashlight up with a trembling hand and lighted Alex's face. "What are you doing?" she whispered.

"I was coming back to get you," Alex said. He put his hand over his face. "Don't shine that in my eyes, you're blinding me."

She shut the light off. "Sorry," Talli began. "I—" A car door slammed. Talli bit off her words and scrambled after Alex into the shadow of the back porch. She stuck her head around the corner, and could just make out a dim form moving toward the front door. "Did you see who it was?" she asked as she turned back to Alex.

He shook his head, the gesture barely visible in the weak light. "I didn't stop to look." He leaned past her. "Was there only one person in the car?"

"I couldn't tell. The headlights were in my eyes."

"They probably saw you. Come on, let's get moving." He stepped away from the house and started jogging back across the damp grass. "Come on," he repeated in a whisper.

Talli started after him. The yard was suddenly bathed in a faint yellow glow as a light clicked on somewhere in the house. She hesitated, turning to look back at the house. The light seemed to be coming from the low rectangular windows of the basement, where she and Alex hadn't looked. She stepped toward the lighted window.

"Talli!" Alex hissed. "What are you doing?"

Talli didn't stop. She took another step toward the window and bent to look in.

At first it was difficult for Talli to make out anything in the basement. The light was dim, and an array of heating ducts and water pipes cluttered the room. The source of the light was a bare bulb that swung from the ceiling. Squinting at the bright area around the bulb,

Talli could make out at least two figures moving around.

One was a man with thick shoulders. It had to be Lynch. Another man went through the pool of light. Talli had an impression that he was very thin, but she didn't get a look at his face. There was a third figure in the shadows on the other side of the bulb. The figure—it was too faint to even say if it was a man or a woman—disappeared into the shadows.

A hand came down on her shoulder, and Talli jumped.

"Talli! Are you completely crazy?" Alex asked.

She shrugged his hand away. "There's somebody down there," she said.

"I know," he said. "That's why I'm trying to get away. Don't you think they saw you when they pulled up?"

"I don't know."

"Well, I do. I think they saw me, and I know they saw you. They're probably calling the police right now."

"Okay," Talli said reluctantly. "Let's go." As she was getting to her feet, a spot of color caught her eye—a scrap of bright red on the floor near the light. It took Talli a moment to realize what it was. She turned to tell Alex about it, but he was already several steps away, trotting toward the gap in the fence.

There was a squeak overhead, followed by a

faint sliding noise. Talli backed away from the house, staring up at the windows above. She couldn't see anything, but she had an overwhelming feeling that something *was* there. Something was watching her.

Talli spun and ran after Alex, squeezing through the loose boards right on his heels. Neither of them spoke as they hurried through the narrow passages and back to Talli's yard. They stood beside the driveway and looked over the fence at the dark bulk of Volker's house.

"There was a purse in the basement," Talli said softly.

"A what?"

"A purse. A red leather purse."

"So?" Alex said. "Maybe Volker likes to play dress up. Still no law against it."

"It reminds me of something," Talli said. "I can't quite put my finger on it, but I know that purse means something."

Alex groaned and shook his head. "How can you know that?"

Talli felt a twinge of anger. "Why are you sticking up for Volker? You've been doing it ever since he got here."

Alex stepped closer to her. "I'm not sticking up for Volker," he said. "I'm watching out for you." He reached a hand inside the hood of her jacket to touch her hair. "I don't want to see you get in trouble."

She leaned her face against his hand for a

moment. "I guess I can't be too mad at you for that," she said, "but I *can* take care of myself."

"That's what you keep telling me," Alex said. He pulled his hand back and smiled. Even in the darkness, she could see his white teeth gleaming. "Okay, Sherlock, now what?" he asked.

"I guess you go home," Talli said.

"Go home?"

She nodded. "My mom will be back soon, and I'm supposed to be inside, studying."

"Boy," he said, "you sure are hard on your assistants. Get them out in the middle of the night, drag them into danger, then toss them away." He gave a loud, theatrical sigh.

Talli pulled him down and gave him a kiss that lasted till the need to breathe broke it off. "Feel better now?" she asked.

"Um hmm. It's always nice to get something for my efforts," he said. "You sure I can't come inside for a while?"

Talli shook her head. "You better not. There's still that triple feature this weekend." She gestured toward his car. "Plenty of time for us to conduct more business then."

Alex walked over to his car and opened the door. "You just make sure that we don't end up spending Saturday night in jail."

"You worry too much."

He laughed as he climbed into the car. "*I* worry too much. Look who's talking!" He drove off with a wave.

As Talli hurried inside, she heard something. She stood peering into the black night, listening. A few minutes later, the sound came again. It was high and thin, and too faint to tell even a direction.

Somewhere in the night, a girl was crying.

Ten

Friday

The morning dawned clear. For the first time in weeks, the clouds parted enough for the low morning sun to shine through Talli's window. She stood in the bright sunshine and stretched. In the strong yellow light, even the upper story of Volker's house looked cheerful. Talli stepped over to her dresser and ran a brush through her hair. Meeting her own eyes in the mirror, she tried out a smile.

Faced with the morning light, Talli found it hard to recall the anxiety that she had felt during the night. So what if Volker kept an empty house? If there was a purse in his basement? If people were walking around in the middle of the night? As Alex had said, none of those things was against the law, and there was probably a simple, reasonable explanation for them all.

Maybe Volker's furniture was stuck in a warehouse somewhere, waiting for the right paperwork. Maybe the purse belonged to a sister, or a daughter, or to someone who had lived in the house before. Maybe the people in the basement were there to work on a leaky pipe. With the sun shining, even the things that had been happening at school seemed unimportant.

Saturday night, she thought. *Dad will be back by then, and he'll take care of everything.* She went downstairs feeling better than she had all week.

Her spirits were boosted further when she reached the bottom of the stairs. There was a rattle of pots and pans from the kitchen and a delicious smell in the air that Talli had almost forgotten. She stepped into the kitchen and found her mother at the stove.

"Good morning," she called.

"Sit down," said Mrs. McAlister, "and get ready for some pancakes."

Talli dropped into a chair and set her book bag on the floor next to her. She stared in wonder at her mother bustling around, pouring batter into a skillet. "Why are you fixing a big breakfast like this?" Talli asked. "You haven't made pancakes in years."

Her mother smiled as she set a plate piled high with pancakes on the table. "I don't know.

I was feeling good this morning, and I thought I would fix something for you."

"Well," said Talli, "you've got enough here for ten people." She speared a pair of pancakes and dropped them on her plate. "How did your meeting go last night?"

"Oh, it was great, just great." Mrs. McAlister brought over a plate of bacon and took a seat across from Talli. "He was great," she said.

Talli froze with a forkful of pancake halfway to her mouth. "He?"

"Did I say he?" Mrs. McAlister looked away, her broad smile still in place. "I suppose I mean your Mr. Volker."

The warmth seemed to go out of the morning. Talli put the bite of pancake in her mouth and chewed it slowly. "You liked him?"

Her mother nodded as she sipped at her coffee. "I'm certainly glad he's come to help us. You know how bad it was getting at your school—gangs, drugs, violence. Your old principal couldn't handle it at all."

"But you think Mr. Volker can?"

"I'm certain of it," said her mother. "He's got so much energy! Everyone at the meeting got so excited." She shook her head, but her smile never wavered. "I've never been at a meeting where everyone was so excited. I think everybody there was ready to listen to him all night."

Talli put her fork down on her plate. The

breakfast that had smelled so good a few minutes before had lost its appeal.

"Everyone likes him?"

"Of course. How could you not like him?" Mrs. McAlister reached across the table and took Talli's hand. "I hate to say it, but I've been afraid for you even to go to school this year." Her eyes were locked on Talli's as she spoke.

"You know, your father and I moved back to this town when you were a baby," she continued. "The main reason was so that you would have a nice place to grow up and go to school."

"I know. Dad gave me the same speech."

"But this year, it was as bad as back in the city." She released Talli's hand and leaned back in her chair. "Now that Mr. Volker's here, I'm not scared at all."

It took Talli a few seconds to find her voice. "That . . . That's good, Mom."

Her mother dug into her breakfast with enthusiasm, downing pancakes and bacon at a furious rate. Talli got up from the table and reached for her book bag. "I'd better get to school."

"But you hardly touched your breakfast!" Mrs. McAlister said. "Are you sure you've had enough?"

"I'm not hungry, I guess. You going to be here tonight?"

"Yes." Mrs. McAlister looked around. "There are so many things that need to be done here. I'm really thinking about doing some serious work around this place."

97

"Okay. I'll see you after school." Talli walked across the room and pulled open the kitchen door.

"Oh, Tallibeth?"

"Yes?"

"If you see your friend Lisa, please tell her I hope her mother is feeling better."

Talli looked back at her mother. "I didn't know Lisa's mom was sick."

Mrs. McAlister nodded. "It happened at the meeting last night. She had some kind of seizure." She shook her head. "She seemed to get over it, but it was really awful." The smile never left her face.

Talli backed out of the house without another word. It took her two tries to get the keys in the ignition of the car. She clenched her fists, trying to control her trembling.

"It could be a coincidence," she whispered into the silent car. "Just because Lisa's mom had some kind of attack, it doesn't mean it has anything to do with what happened to Ashley Westin at school." Talli pounded her hand against the steering wheel. The two attacks *were* related, she was certain of that. The connection was Volker.

Talli shifted the car out of the driveway and headed for Lisa's house. They were running late, and they barely had a chance to exchange a word as Talli sped through town.

Talli was surprised to find several open slots

in the school parking lot. She parked the Pinto and they headed for the front door as Volker's car slid into his reserved slot next to the school. Talli paused, her hand gripping the metal handle of the door, as the principal climbed out and began to walk stiffly toward her.

"Today he looks as old as you made him sound," Lisa whispered.

The morning sun brought out the deep grooves in Volker's face. A hint of bare scalp showed through his silver hair, and even his gray suit looked shabby in the sunlight. As strong as he had looked in the shadows of the auditorium, he looked old and run-down in the daylight.

"Ms. McAlister, Ms. Taylor," he said as he approached. "How are you this morning?"

"Fine," said Talli. Lisa held the door open for him. For just a moment, Talli remembered the headlights of Volker's car, pinning her to the front of his house in a circle of light. Had Volker recognized her?

But Volker didn't act as if he knew anything about her nighttime visit to his house. He nodded his head toward Lisa, and walked off in the direction his office without another word. His movement was so wooden that Talli wondered if he was having trouble with something like arthritis.

Talli let out a breath that she didn't realize she had been holding, and followed Lisa into the school. She pushed her way through the halls. As always, they were crowded, but like the parking lot outside, they seemed less crowded than they had the day before. As soon as Talli reached her homeroom, the teacher handed her a note. Puzzled, Talli unfolded it to find a message telling her to come to the office.

Talli felt as though she had swallowed a brick. Alex was right—she *had* been seen. She got up from her seat and started for the hallway. Her legs and feet were numb as she walked out the door and down the hallway. Even the noise of the crowd seemed distant. Talli stepped into the outer office and started across the room toward the closed door to Volker's private room.

"You can't go in there," said a voice at her elbow.

Talli almost jumped out of her skin. She had completely forgotten about the secretary that worked in the office. The expression on the woman's round face was as sour as green apples, which was typical for her. In almost four years of high school, Talli had never learned the secretary's name.

"I'm supposed to see Mr. Volker," Talli said.

The secretary shoved her thick glasses up on her nose with one pudgy finger. "Mr. Volker is busy," she replied. "What's this about?"

Talli showed her the note. "It said to come right away."

"Oh, you must be Elizabeth McAlister," said the secretary.

"Tallibeth."

The woman blinked behind her glasses. "What's that?"

"My name is Tallibeth."

"Whatever. You don't need to see Mr. Volker. I know what this is all about."

Now it was Talli's turn to blink. "I don't understand," she said. But whatever was going on, the idea that she wouldn't have to be alone with Volker was a great relief.

"The police were here this morning," said the secretary. "It seems that a student named . . ." She stopped to pull some papers from a desk littered with folders, cups of pencils, and a hefty key ring. ". . . Samantha Deveraux is missing."

"She is?"

"They talked to several students, and your name came up as someone that was close to her." She stopped and looked up at Talli. "Is there any information you can provide on Samantha Deveraux's location?"

Close to Samantha? Talli thought. *How could anyone think I was close to Samantha?* But she had to admit that, no matter how many guys were crawling after her, Samantha didn't seem to have a group of close friends. Talli hated to think that perhaps she *was* as close to Samantha as anyone.

"I talked to her before first period yesterday," said Talli. "She was supposed to meet me after school. I waited for her, but she didn't show up."

The secretary scribbled on her papers. "Is that all?"

"That's all I know."

"Was she upset? Did she talk about going somewhere?"

"I'm sorry," said Talli. "I didn't really know her that well." Suddenly Talli realized she was talking about Samantha as if she were dead, not missing.

The secretary's face settled back to its usual frown. "I see," she said. "You can go back to class. If the police need anything more, they can talk to you themselves." She began to type.

Talli glanced again at the door that separated Volker's office from the secretary's area. It was just a blank wooden door. There was a slightly darker square where the previous principal's nameplate had been attached. Volker had not put up a new nameplate.

Suddenly a glimmer of green light flickered under the door. It was the same verdant, pulsing light that she and Alex had seen lighting up the school. There was a soft groan from someone in the office. It didn't sound like Volker.

Talli looked at the secretary, but the woman only continued to type, plinking out her words with a pace as monotonous as a slow drip. If she heard the noise, or noticed the light from the inner office, she gave no sign.

Then Talli noticed the key ring on the desk. It was large, with at least two dozen keys, and a flat piece of dark metal for a grip. It didn't look like the kind of ring that a woman would use for her personal keys. It had an industrial, heavy-duty look.

Quickly, not even sure why she was doing it, Talli reached out and grabbed the ring. She flinched as some of the keys jangled. Holding it against her side, and trying to hide it in her hand, Talli walked quickly out of the office. She was two steps down the hall when the secretary called after her.

"McAlister!"

Preparing herself for the worst, Talli turned back. "Yes?"

The secretary was leaning from the door of the office. Talli started to raise the key ring, wondering what they would do to her for stealing it.

"What did you say your first name was?" asked the woman.

Talli almost laughed in relief. "Tallibeth," she said.

"With a 'y'?"

"An 'i.'"

"Humph," grunted the woman. "Funny name."

She went back into the office, and Talli hurried to her class with the key ring still clutched in her hand. The bell rang before she was even back to her desk, and Talli had to scurry to gather her things and head off to her first-period class.

In the hallway, she caught up to Lisa and pulled her aside. "Samantha's missing," she said.

"She probably couldn't come to school without the proper nail polish," Lisa replied.

Talli shook her head. "No, she's really missing. The police have been looking for her and everything."

"Yeah? That's weird. I heard that a couple of other kids were missing."

"Like who?"

"Like Cheryl Fellini and Paul Katz," said Lisa. "I heard that the police are looking for them, too."

"Cheryl and Paul," repeated Talli. "Didn't they both go to Volker's office this week? Right before Ashley got sick?"

Lisa shrugged. "I guess so. Why? Do you think that had something to do with it?"

Talli nodded. "A lot of kids got sent to the office in the last couple of days. I wonder how many of them are missing."

"You think Volker's collecting them in his basement or something?" Lisa arched her eyebrows dramatically. "Maybe he's selling them?"

"This is serious, Lisa. Last night, when Alex and I went over to Volker's house, we—"

"Wait. When you went *where*?"

"Volker's house," said Talli. "Alex and I went over there last night while my mom was at the PTO meeting."

Lisa shook her head. "Alex went along with

this? Talli, you've got to stop this before you get in trouble."

"Don't you understand?" asked Talli. "People are missing. People we know. And I think Volker is behind it."

The skepticism faded from Lisa's face. "I guess the scary thing is that I believe you," she said. "I don't want to, but there *is* something about Volker that bothers me." She closed her eyes and took a deep breath. "All right," she said. "What do we do now?"

"I've got a plan," Talli said. "Meet me in the prop room last period."

Eleven

The hallways behind the stage were as dim as they had been on Tuesday. Talli had never thought about it before, but it was actually kind of creepy in that dark place.

"So," Lisa said. "Are you going to tell me the great plan now? I've been waiting all day."

Talli looked down the hall at the empty stage. Remembering how Volker had moved in and out of the darkness as he disarmed the three guys on Tuesday, it was easy to believe he might be hiding out there again. "Let's go into the prop room," she said. "I'll tell you there."

They stepped around the painted scenery of Hamlet's castle. Talli carefully closed the door behind them.

Lisa peeked around behind the flat sheets of canvas. "Nobody hiding back here," she said.

"All right," Talli said. "Last night Alex and I went over to Volker's house."

"You said that already. What did you see?"

"Not much. The house was empty."

"That's what made you so sure Volker's behind everything?"

"No. I guess it was my mom that started me on—" She stopped. "That reminds me, how is your mother?"

"My mother?" Lisa raised her eyebrows in puzzlement. "She's fine. Why shouldn't she be?"

"My mom said that she had some kind of seizure at the PTO meeting last night."

Lisa shook her head. "There's nothing wrong with my mother."

"But my mom made it sound like something really bad. Something like what happened to Ashley in class."

"No way," Lisa said. "In fact, the only weird thing was that she was up early this morning—"

"Making breakfast?" guessed Talli.

"No. Cleaning the house. She was all over the place at six A.M. Dusting, cleaning. She was really wound up."

"My mom was making breakfast," Talli said. She looked into one of the gray paintings of a castle wall and frowned. "Why would she say there was something wrong with your mother if there wasn't? She asked me to tell you that she hoped your mom got better."

"Well," Lisa said, "if there was anything

107

wrong, my mom sure didn't mention it."

Talli tilted her head to the side and looked at Lisa thoughtfully. "Does your mother usually clean a lot?"

"My mom? Come on, Talli. You've seen my house. My mom's so busy at her job that she gave up on housework a long time ago."

"My mother was fixing pancakes this morning. First time she's made a hot breakfast in ten years."

Lisa leaned back against a section of painted wall. "So you think Volker's replaced our moms with pod people?"

"I think he's done *something* to them," Talli said. "Did your mom say anything about Volker this morning?"

Lisa rolled her eyes toward the ceiling. "Yeah, she thinks he hung the stars. She thinks Volker is going to protect all us awful kids from our awful selves."

"My mom said about the same thing." Talli stepped closer to her friend. "Don't you think that's weird? That they would like him so much?"

"I think it's all weird, Talli," Lisa said. "I never said it wasn't weird. I can't figure out why Volker would do any of the things you think he's done, though. What's he got to gain?"

"Remember what Alex said? Maybe Volker's doing drugs."

"You think he spiked the punch at the PTO meeting?"

"Maybe," Talli said. "It might be why they were acting so strange this morning."

Lisa slid down the backdrop till she was sitting on the dusty floor. "I hate to tell you this, but drug dealers don't generally kidnap people. Why would Volker make off with Samantha or Cheryl?"

"I don't know," Talli said. She sat on the floor next to Lisa. "But tonight, I think we can find out."

"You and Alex already went to his house and found nothing."

Talli reached into her book bag and pulled out the ring of keys. "We checked his house," she said, "but we didn't check his office."

Lisa's eyes bulged as she looked at the key ring. "Is that what I think it is?"

"I took it from Volker's secretary." Talli held the keys in front of Lisa and rattled them. "Will you help me?"

"Talli, I think you're about to help yourself into juvenile hall." Lisa sighed. "But I guess I might as well go with you. Okay, what's our strategy?"

Glancing at the door to make sure it was still closed, Talli laid out her plan. "We'll drive over here after it's dark," she said. "I'll get into the school, then you'll take my car back home and wait."

"Wait for what?" Lisa asked. "Why do I take your car?"

"You take it back to my street so you can watch Volker's house. If you see him leave his house, you let me know so I can get out of here."

"How can I let you know anything if I'm back at your house, and you're in school?"

"My dad's got a couple of police radios at home," Talli said. "I'll borrow them. You take one so you can signal me."

"Wow. This is beginning to sound like something on TV."

"Anyway, as soon as I get a look around his office and get back out, I'll signal you to come get me."

"What do you expect to find in his office?"

"I don't know," Talli said. "Something. Anything that will explain what's going on."

There was a long silence. "Well," Talli said at last, "do you think it will work?"

"If you mean getting into his office," Lisa said, "then yes, I think it will work. That's not what I'm worried about."

"What are you worried about?"

"What if you're right?" she asked. "What if Volker is behind everything that's been going on? What do we do then?"

"Then we go to the police," Talli said.

Lisa shook her head. "If he's behind it all, I don't think it's the kind of thing you can go to the police about."

"What do you mean?"

Lisa stood and walked across the narrow

room. "I don't know," she said. She wrapped her arms around herself and shivered. "All I know is that the longer you talk, the more frightened I get."

Talli got up and brushed dust from the legs and seat of her jeans. "I'm the one that reads all the horror novels. Have you been sneaking them in while I wasn't looking?"

"I'm not kidding. I'm really starting to get a bad feeling about this."

"You?" Talli said. "No kidding! Now I *know* we're in trouble."

Lisa's lips turned up in a slow smile. "All right. I suppose I have been giving you a hard time this week. From now on, I'll be good."

The final bell rang, announcing the end of the school day. The sound of students hurrying through the halls was like distant thunder. Talli reached down for her book bag. "You think you'll have any trouble getting permission for tonight?"

"I haven't had a date in six weeks," Lisa said. "If I tell my mom that a guy called, she'll shove me out the door before I can even finish explaining."

Talli laughed. "Okay, let's get home and start getting ready. I want to make sure everything is in the car and waiting when we need it."

They stepped out of the prop room and walked through the passage behind the stage, their sneakers squeaking across the wooden floor. The doors at the top of the auditorium were open, and they could see students passing down the halls on their way out of the school.

"Wait a sec," Talli said. "I left my coat in my locker."

"Okay," Lisa said. "I think I'll go on out to the car. I want to get some of this sunshine while I can."

"See you there in five minutes." Talli turned back down the long hallway that led to her locker. There was a male student trying to get into a locker a few doors from hers. As she pulled out her coat, Talli saw him drop the combination lock and pound his fist against the metal door.

"Having trouble?" she asked.

He turned to face her. She didn't recognize him at first. His skin was a pale waxy gray, and his eyes were sunken in rings of flesh so dark it looked bruised. Only the straggling straw-yellow hair looked the same. It was Morris South.

Without thinking, Talli took a half-step back.

Morris blinked at her, but his eyes seemed unfocused. "Trouble," he said. His voice was thick and rubbery. He licked at his split lips. "No trouble." There was an unpleasant odor around him, an odor that made Talli feel ill. It smelled like mildew, and things gone bad in the bottom of the refrigerator. She remembered the shadowy figures in Volker's basement. The thin-

112

ner one was the same size as Morris.

"Good," Talli said. She reached out and pushed her own locker closed. "I guess I'll be going."

Morris stepped toward her, and Talli took another hasty step back. "I know you," he said. "You were there."

"I've got to go," Talli said.

"You were there when *he* came." Morris nodded. A dull light glowed in his cloudy eyes. He reached out for her, but his motions were slow and clumsy. Talli dodged his grasp and backed away down the hall.

The one attempt at grabbing her seemed to take all the energy out of Morris. He slumped against the line of lockers. "Tell him I'm waiting," he said. "Will you tell him that?"

"Okay," Talli said. "I'll tell him."

Moving as slowly as a man underwater, Morris shuffled back to his locker and began laboriously dialing the combination. Talli watched him for a few seconds, then hurried out of the school. She was tremendously glad to get out in the sunshine. She stood on the concrete outside the door for a few minutes, just breathing, trying to get the stench that had surrounded Morris cleaned out of her lungs. When she felt a little steadier, she trotted across the parking lot.

"It's about time," Lisa said as Talli approached the car. "I was beginning—" She stopped and tilted her head to one side. "You okay?" she asked.

Talli nodded. "I just ran into Morris South."

"Morris South! The guy from the prop room?"

"Uh-huh. He looked like a zombie. Whatever Volker's giving people, I think Morris is really, really hooked." She opened the car door, climbed in, and leaned over to unlock Lisa's door.

They were quiet as they drove out of the lot and through the town. The slanting afternoon sunshine painted the fronts of the houses and stores red-gold. The shoppers along the street had shed their heavy coats in favor of light jackets. It almost looked like spring.

"It's supposed to snow tonight," Lisa said as she looked out her window. "Hard to believe."

"Let's hope it doesn't snow too much," Talli said. "I don't want to be making a high-speed escape in the middle of a blizzard."

"I don't want to be making high-speed escapes at all!" Lisa replied.

Talli dropped Lisa off, then headed for home. She was glad that her mother worked late on Thursdays—Talli didn't want to explain what she was planning for tonight. But when she pulled into her driveway, she was surprised to see her mother's car waiting.

"Mom?" Talli called as she came through the back door. "You home?"

There was no answer, but Talli found her mother's purse and coat on the kitchen table. "Mom?" she called again.

114

There was a muffled answer from above, and Talli hurried up the steps to her mother's bedroom. "You in there, Mom?" she said. She pushed open the door.

The room was dark, and Talli strained to see. "Mom?"

"Tallibeth," said a soft voice.

Talli hesitated at the door, unsure if the voice was her mother's, but as her eyes adapted to the dim light, she saw the huddled form under the blankets. "Mom! What's wrong?" She hurried to the bed. Her mother's features looked pale and drawn.

Mrs. McAlister moved weakly. "I'm so cold," she said. "I got so cold at work, and so, so tired. I had to come home and rest."

Talli laid her hand against her mother's forehead. There was no fever that Talli could feel. In fact, her mother's skin was icy. "You think you've got the flu?" she asked.

"Maybe," Mrs. McAlister mumbled. "I think I need some rest."

"I'll get the thermometer." Talli reached for the lamp beside the bed and snapped on the light.

At once her mother sat stiffly upright. She flung out an arm and sent the lamp flying off the table. There was a bang as the lamp bounced against the wall, and a crash as the glass base shattered on the floor. "No light!" she screamed. She drew several ragged breaths while Talli

115

looked at her in shock, then she settled back into the covers. "It hurts my eyes," she finished in a whisper.

"Sure, Mom," Talli said. She backed toward the door. "How about I fix something for supper?"

"No supper."

"I'll fix a can of soup. Soup is good when you're not feeling well."

"No supper," her mother repeated. "I don't feel like eating anything."

"Get some rest, then."

"Yes," Mrs. McAlister said. She rolled over and buried her ashen face in the pillow. She mumbled something else, but Talli couldn't make it out.

Talli left the room, her shoes crunching on bits of shattered glass as she walked. She closed the door behind her. In the hallway, she found her throat growing tight. Whatever was wrong with her mother, it wasn't the flu. It was something terribly worse.

She wondered if she should call the doctor. She'd never had to make a decision like that before. It had always been her mother who called the doctor about Talli. More than ever, she wished her father were home.

Whatever it was that her mother had, there was no doubt about one thing: the lean, sickly look on her mother's face was the same look she had seen on the face of Morris South.

Whatever he's given them, Talli thought, *it must be really bad.*

116

But even as Talli was thinking this, she didn't believe a word of it. Other people might be afraid of drug dealers, but Talli's mind had never worked that way. Right from the start, she hadn't really thought Volker was a drug dealer. She didn't think he had connections with the mob, or a basement full of Baggies and needles.

What she suspected, deep down, was something that most of the students at Westerberg High would have laughed at. She suspected that Volker was something that she had no name for. Something she couldn't describe.

She felt that the principal was no more human than the owls that slipped through the air on cold winter nights, or the worms that plowed the rich earth of old graveyards. She had felt that way ever since she saw his hands coming out of the darkness to dash away the guys with knives.

He hadn't done it to protect her or Lisa. Like a lion driving the jackals from their feed, Volker was only saving the kill for himself.

Talli walked over to the window and looked out at Volker's house. The sun had already sunk below the horizon, leaving the ground in darkness, but the upper edge of Volker's house was still tinted by a bloody red light. Talli clenched her fists and went in search of her father's police radios.

The night was coming on fast. Talli wanted to be ready.

Twelve

"How do you work this thing?" Lisa asked. She turned the gray plastic radio over in her hands, looking at the profusion of small dials and buttons.

"Ignore most of it," Talli said. "The only button to worry about is this one." She pointed to a large red button on the front of the device. "Press that one when you want to talk, but remember to let go when you're done, or you won't hear me."

"What about the channel? Do we need to set that?"

"I already did. Make sure you don't change it. This thing's not like a regular walkie-talkie. It picks up only four channels. Two of them are for the local police and ambulance. One is the state police station. The other one's not being used yet. That's the one we'll talk on." She tapped at the dial on the front of the radio. "If we talk on any of the other channels, some policeman's bound to hear us."

"Maybe that's not such a bad thing," Lisa said. "We may need help from the police."

"I'll keep it in mind," Talli said, "but I don't particularly want to call the police when I'm breaking into a building."

She looked through the windshield at the darkened school. They were parked in the same place where she and Alex had watched Volker lead Morris South out of the school. Tonight there was no sign of anyone else near the school. True to Lisa's predictions, the temperature had already dropped ten degrees since sunset, and fat snowflakes were beginning to drift down out of the darkness. "It's time for me to go," Talli said.

"Are you sure?" Lisa asked. "I mean, we don't have to do this. Your dad will be home in a couple of days."

"How was your mom tonight?"

"About as sick as you said your mom was." Lisa ran a hand through her thick brown hair. "Okay, I get the point."

"We'll pull around behind the auditorium. The doors there are out of sight from the road. If we go in and out that way, no one will see us."

Talli killed the lights as she drove along the school parking lot. It was eerie to drive the car through the darkness. The thickening fall of snow, so white in the glow of the headlights, seemed black as coal with the lights out. The tires squeaked as they rolled across the thin layer of snow that already blanketed the empty parking lot. Talli eased around the corner of the school and pulled up near the double doors that were usually opened only for plays.

"Is it okay to turn on the lights once I get away from the school?" Lisa asked. "I wouldn't want to run into somebody."

"Turn them on when you get to the edge of the parking lot," Talli said. She pushed open her car door, and a blast of cold air filled the car. Snowflakes swirled in and melted against the dashboard. "I'm outta here," she said.

Lisa leaned across the gap between the seats and grabbed Talli in a quick hug. "Be careful."

Talli took a firm grip on the radio and stepped out of the car. The snow was slippery underfoot. She hadn't thought to change into boots, and she almost fell making it to the auditorium door. She pulled the key ring from her coat pocket and tried a key in the door. No luck. There were close to fifty keys on the ring, and Talli worried that she would have to try them all before getting in. There might not even *be* a key to this door on the ring. Then the third key she tried fit into the lock and turned with a solid click.

Talli pulled on the door, and it opened into

darkness. She glanced back at the car for a minute. She could see Lisa moving into the driver's seat, and the wipers beating at the snow. She turned and stepped into the auditorium, letting the door fall closed behind her.

As soon as it closed, Talli was swallowed by blackness as thick as velvet. With no windows and no lights on, the inside of the auditorium was utterly black. Sparks danced in front of Talli's eyes, and she stepped forward carefully. She wished she had thought to bring a flashlight. Her plan for looking in Volker's office had seemed so well thought out when she had explained it to Lisa. Thirty seconds into the plan, and she'd already thought of two things she'd forgotten.

Talli thought for a moment about turning on the lights, but she was afraid that someone might see them under the door from outside. So she walked slowly into the darkness, waving her hand in front of her like a blind woman, until she bumped up against the first row of seats. Talli knew that the door she had come through was near the base of the stage. Keeping one hand on the seats, she followed them up the gentle slope to the top row.

A faint light leaked from under the doors in the lobby, so Talli had no trouble crossing the empty space. She stopped at the door and listened for a moment, but there was nothing to hear. She eased a door open and peered down the hall.

The light came from tiny emergency lights spaced over each doorway. It was faint, but after the complete darkness of the auditorium, Talli's eyes were well adapted to little light. She stepped out into the hallway and walked along the worn carpet. The lights made a soft buzzing sound, but except for that, the school was silent. Talli passed between the rows of lockers and the shut doors of the classrooms.

There was another light in the outer room of Volker's office. A desk lamp glowed from the table where Talli had taken the key ring. It took her ten tries to find the key that would admit her to the outer office, but at least there was enough light to see the doorknob. Then she had to try five more keys to get Volker's door open. It was dark inside. Talli stepped through and closed the door behind her before turning on the light.

She was not really surprised to see that Volker's office looked completely normal. After all, dozens of students had been in there; it couldn't be too weird. Still, it was disappointing. An old metal desk in the center of the room was strewn with manila folders, and flanked by a dull-gray filing cabinet. Behind it was a low table covered in dusty magazines.

There were ceiling fixtures in the room, but no light came from them. The only illumination was from a floor lamp shoved back in one corner. Two straight-backed chairs sat by the lamp in a puddle of light. Talli assumed that the chairs were where Volker placed those students who had to see him in the office.

Turning to the desk, Talli pulled open the wide center drawer. A collection of pens rolled loose in the bottom of the drawer over a scattering of paper clips. There was nothing else. She grabbed one of the smaller drawers on the side and jerked it open. It was empty. So was the next drawer. And the next. The desk was as empty and featureless as Volker's house.

Talli straightened up and sighed. She wasn't going to learn anything here. She hadn't been sure what to look for, but clearly the office was clean. Talli glanced at the folders on the desk. Each seemed to contain only a few sheets of paper. At the top of each folder was a tab with a name typed onto a yellow label. Student folders; not a surprising thing to find on the desk of the principal.

The name on one of the folders caught Talli's eye—"Paul Michael Katz." She looked at the stack more closely, and found another familiar name, "Cheryl Jean Fellini." Feeling rather guilty about peeking into another student's file, Talli put her radio down on the desk, picked up Cheryl's folder, and flipped it open.

Inside were pages of preprinted forms spotted with the results of all the standardized tests Cheryl had taken over the years. In a glance, Talli could see how Cheryl had progressed from grade school to senior year. At the very bottom of the page, a few words were scrawled in red.

"Very sensitive," said the note. "Will progress rapidly."

Talli frowned at the words. They didn't sound *too* different from the kinds of things that principals and school counselors were always saying, but the phrasing seemed odd.

Talli put down Cheryl's folder and took the next one from the stack. She almost dropped it when she saw the name at the top. "Samantha Diane Deveraux."

Talli flipped open Samantha's folder. The dots and jiggles that represented Samantha's scholastic scores were much better than Talli would have expected. Perhaps Samantha's blond-ditz act really was an act. There was no writing at the bottom of the first page. Talli flipped it over. On the back was the expected note: "Her vanity will be her undoing."

Talli repeated the words quietly. Even more than what was in Cheryl's folder, this little observation struck a wrong chord. What school principal had ever written an official note about a student's vanity? It sounded more like something that a bad preacher might have said. She closed Samantha's folder.

Samantha's name had been surprising, but the name on the next folder made Talli gasp. She reached down and snatched up the folder labeled "Morris Bateman South." Talli had to flip several pages of the green tinted paper before she came to the expected note. "An outsider," it said. "Bring him inside."

Again, the words weren't definite enough to prove that anything was really wrong. Volker could have been going over the records of students he was concerned about, writing his observations in the folders.

Talli dropped the folder and picked up the next. She didn't recognize the name, but there was another note at the end, more words that could have many meanings. She went through one folder after another, quickly reading the notes, and barely glancing at the names on the folders.

Near the bottom of the stack was a folder that featured a very familiar name, "Lisa Marie Taylor." Talli opened it slowly, feeling again the guilt of looking someplace she shouldn't be. The note was on the first page. "A follower," read the stiff red letters. "Give her something new to follow."

There was a beep from the radio, and Talli dropped the folder. Pale green paper went skidding from the desk and onto the floor.

"Talli? Talli! You there?" said Lisa's static-laden voice through the tiny radio speaker. "Talli?"

Talli grabbed the radio and pushed the talk button. "I'm here," she said. "What's wrong?" When she released the button, Lisa's voice came back at once.

125

". . . alli? Answer, please."

"Let off the button, Lisa!" Talli said in frustration. There was no way that Lisa could hear her as long as she was pushing the talk button on her radio.

"Talli, they're coming!" Lisa cried. "Volker's car just left. If you can hear me, get out!" There was a sudden squeak of interference, and Lisa's voice disappeared.

Talli pressed the button on her radio again. "Lisa?" she called, and released the button. No answer came. She tried again, but no matter how far she turned up the volume, there was nothing but the white noise of background static.

Frantic, Talli looked around the office. Dropping the radio on the desk, she grabbed the scattered papers of Lisa's file from the floor and shoved the loose sheets into the folder. As she put it back on the desk, the name on the very last folder caught her eye.

"Tallibeth McAlister."

Talli's fingers trembled as she opened the cover of her own folder. There was nothing on the first page, or the second. For a moment, she thought that Volker had left no note. On the bottom of the third and final page she found it. Unlike the other folders, Talli's had only a single word. In tall hard letters, it said, "Dangerous."

Thirteen

Talli could feel her heart beating faster as she closed her folder and put Lisa's on top. Moving as fast as she could, she tried to restack the folders in the order she had found them. With a final glance around the office to make sure that nothing was out of place, Talli snatched up her radio and left.

She flipped the light off on her way out. The outer office door locked with a key. Talli was searching for a key that fit when she heard a door open somewhere else in the building.

Without checking to see if the door had locked, Talli jerked the key ring loose and ran for the auditorium. Her own footsteps were terrifyingly loud in her ears as she sprinted down the hall. The hallway seemed darker than ever, every turn leading her into deeper gloom.

She stopped at the door to the auditorium lobby, and tried to hold her breath. At first she heard nothing, but then there was a distant shuffling sound. Far down the hallway, something banged against the lockers. There was a long, sliding noise, and a deep groan of metal. It sounded as if an elephant were trying to squeeze its way down the narrow hall. Then the shuffling noise started again. It was louder, and closer.

Talli slipped into the lobby. The blackness was more complete than ever. She stumbled forward, blundering into the wall, and having to feel along the bumpy plasterboard to find the door into the auditorium itself.

She got her hand on the first of the seats, feeling the coarse tweedy fabric under her fingers, and started down the slope to the exit. Inside, a voice shouted at her to run, but she tried to stay calm. Running on this slanting floor in complete darkness would guarantee disaster.

The lobby door swung open. There was a moment of light as the door opened, then it was blocked out by a form in the doorway. In that second, Talli saw that she was no more than a third of the way to the door where she had come in. She dived into the seats as the door swung closed, pressing her face against the sticky concrete floor. She fought to control her breathing.

There was movement in the lobby, a soft sound, like something being dragged across the

128

carpet. The sound grew closer as the thing moved out of the lobby and into the top of the auditorium.

Then another sound began. A squeak followed by a thump. It happened again, squeak-thump, and again. It took several more repetitions before Talli figured out what the sound was. Whoever—whatever—was in the auditorium, it was moving from one row to the next, flipping down the seats and letting them spring up against the padded backs.

Talli inched forward on elbows and toes. She still had the key ring in one hand and the police radio in the other. Every time the keys banged together, she winced, but she kept moving. Behind her the squeak-thump of rising and falling chair seats grew closer.

She reached the center aisle about the same time that the noises reached the row in which she was crawling. Talli got to her knees and began to crawl quickly down the sloping aisle.

The thing in the darkness screamed. It had to be a thing, because no human throat was capable of that long, tearing metal screech. Talli sprang to her feet and ran, tumbling into the next section of chairs. The key ring fell from her hand and went sliding off along the floor. Talli got up, took another step, and fell again.

Behind her there was a horrible commotion as what sounded like a dozen people tried to shove through the seats at once. There was a crash that sounded like an entire row of seats being overturned.

Talli crawled, and ran, and fell through the seats. When she smashed into the wall on the other side, she couldn't help but scream. She fumbled along the wall, searching for the door. Another sound joined the cacophony behind her, a high-pitched, grating whine. The sound surged as the thing moved across the aisle and plunged into the second section of seats. It was moving faster now, rushing down on Talli in the velvet darkness. The door seemed to have disappeared. Talli felt along yard after yard of concrete without a sign of an opening. The thing was right behind her. She thought she could feel its breath on the back of her neck.

Talli's hand came down on a row of switches. She didn't hesitate. As bad as it might be to be discovered here, it couldn't be worse than spending one more second in the darkness with whatever was behind her. Talli flipped the whole bank of switches with a sweep of her hand.

Lights sprang on all over the auditorium. Stage lights, lights along the aisles, lights along the walls. Talli spun to face her pursuer.

There was nothing. The room was completely empty. There was no slobbering monster, no row of overturned chairs. Nothing.

Talli's legs felt so weak that she would have fallen without the wall to lean on. With no thought of turning out the lights, she moved slowly to the door. She pushed against the opening bar with her back. Her eyes kept scanning the rows of seats for movement. There was nothing. All the noises had given way to silence. Talli eased out into the night and let the door shut on the empty auditorium.

She staggered away from the door into a drift of snow that came halfway to her knees. She hadn't noticed the tears on her cheeks until the cold air started to freeze them. The snow was falling so thick and heavy, whirling around in the space behind the building, that it was almost like being inside a tornado of white. There was no sign of Lisa or of Talli's car.

Talli held up the police radio and turned up the dial. The familiar static sounded warm over the whistling wind. It still seemed to be working.

She pushed the talk button. "Lisa? Talk to me, Lisa." She released the button and pressed her ear to the speaker. There was something there, the very faint chatter of some distant police station on the same channel. There was nothing from Lisa.

Talli spent five minutes trying to reach Lisa. She flipped the radio over to the local police band for a moment, and listened in to the sound of the officers patrolling the burger places on the other side of town. Then she flipped back to the station that Lisa should be using. Silence.

Could something be wrong with Lisa's radio?

Or maybe Talli's radio wasn't actually transmitting. She wished they had tested them. Talli had meant to check the radio as soon as she got inside the school, but she had forgotten.

"A great plan," Talli mumbled. "One really, really great plan."

She stepped away from the building, blinking snowflakes from her eyes. The tracks she had made getting in had been obscured by the new snow. Talli walked around the corner of the building and was met by a blast of cold air. The parking lot was empty. There were no cars in sight, and no tracks in the parking lot.

Talli shivered. She wasn't dressed to face a blizzard. It was over two miles back to her house, and at this hour, nothing on this side of Westerberg would be open. She looked back at the school. The auditorium door was still unlocked; she could always go back inside and wait there.

It didn't take her very long to reach a decision. She buttoned her coat and began to walk.

Her feet were freezing before she even made it out of the parking lot. Her hands and face weren't far behind. She had to shove the police radio in her pocket and cover her hands. She wasn't sure if she could hear Lisa with the radio stored away, but she was sure that her fingers wouldn't stand up to holding it out in the open much longer.

There were few houses between the school and the main part of town, but there were plenty of trees. Talli watched them suspiciously. The shadows under their empty branches were almost as dark as the inside of the auditorium, and she couldn't shake the conviction that *something* had been after her in the black place. If she hadn't turned on those lights, would it have gotten her, or had it been nothing more than noise?

A new blast of north wind came whistling along the street. Talli hunched her shoulders as her hair blew into her face. The snow seemed to grow deeper by the minute. Downtown Westerberg was empty. A few cars passed by, but Talli didn't recognize them. She was tempted to wave someone down, but she didn't want to take the chance that the car she stopped might belong to Volker. Besides, even in a small town like Westerberg, it wasn't a good idea for a teenage girl to hop into a strange car at night.

She passed the only stoplight in the downtown area, and started down the long hill that led into the subdivision where she lived. The houses along the hill were old, relics of Civil War times, and their yards were filled with shadows cast by thick oak and hickory trees. This section of the street was well-lit by frequent streetlamps, but that only made the gloom of the yards seem deeper. Talli was glad when she reached the bottom of the hill and turned off the main street into the newer section of town where her house was located.

Her feet were beyond frozen. They were stinging so badly that she could barely walk. Her cheeks and nose felt as raw as ground beef, but she was almost home. Soon she could sit at the kitchen table with Lisa and down some hot chocolate. They could talk, and work out what to do next. Memories of what had happened in the auditorium started to rise in her mind, but Talli shoved them down. When she was warm, dry, and inside her own home, *then* she would think about it.

Talli stepped into the road, and walked in the groove left behind by some passing car. She pulled a hand from her pocket and glanced at her watch. After ten o'clock. It had taken an hour to walk the two miles from school. She hoped Lisa would still be waiting, and hadn't taken off for the school by some other route. When she turned the final corner, and saw her car parked in front of her house, Talli drew a huge sigh of relief.

Talli headed straight for the car. As she approached it, she saw the soft glow of the dome light between the front seats. The passenger door was ajar, and a yellow rectangle of light spilled out onto the snow.

Talli yanked open the door and leaned in. "You made me walk—" she started. But she never finished her sentence. The police radio lay on the passenger seat. The keys dangled from the ignition. But Lisa was not in the car.

Talli leaned back, looking at the ground for a clue. There was not a single track in the snow. Except for the footprints she had made coming down the street, it was smooth and unbroken in all directions.

Lisa was gone.

Fourteen

Brilliant beams of blue shot out into the night, bouncing from the snow and gleaming from houses as the bubble lights on the police car turned slowly round and round. Talli watched as Sergeant Lansky shone his flashlight around her car. "You say you were at the school?" he asked as he leaned in to look at the floorboard.

"That's right," Talli said. Her feet, which had barely thawed while she waited in her house for Sergeant Lansky to arrive, were beginning to freeze again.

"What were you doing over there at this hour of night?"

"I told you already," she said. "I was working on props for a play. Lisa was supposed to come pick me up."

Sergeant Lansky pulled out a small notebook

and glanced at it. "But she was in your car," he said. "Why was that?"

"She wanted to go get something," Talli said.

The policeman nodded. He put his pen in his mouth and hummed to himself as he turned the pages. Shutting the book, he took the pen and jammed it into his jacket pocket. "When she didn't show up, you decided to walk home. And you found your car back here, empty." He looked up and gave her a cold smile. "And then you called the station."

"That's right," Talli said. She watched as Sergeant Lansky slowly circled the car, his eyes on the ground. She had the feeling that the policeman didn't believe her. And, of course, she *was* lying. But if she told him that she had been at the school to break into Volker's office, and that Lisa's purpose in waiting in the car was to spy on the principal, she knew he'd have her down at the police station in ten seconds flat.

Sergeant Lansky finished his circle of the car. He shoved his notepad into the pocket after his pencil, and zipped up his jacket. "I don't see any signs of a struggle," he said.

"Lisa's missing," Talli said. "Isn't that enough?"

The policeman shook his head. "She's only been gone for, what? Two hours? There's no way I can file a missing person report."

"Even with all the other missing kids?"

"Like who?"

"Like Samantha Deveraux, or Cheryl Fellini, or—"

Sergeant Lansky waved a black-gloved hand through the frigid air. "We already have a good tip on them. Got a report in this morning that two of them were seen up near Chicago." He stepped past Talli and opened the door of the police cruiser.

"You can't just leave," she said. "What about Lisa?"

"I can't file a missing person yet," Sergeant Lansky said. He gave Talli another of his sharklike smiles. "You should know that. I don't know what you're up to, Ms. McAlister." He pronounced "Ms." like a noise a fly would make. "But I know that you're not telling me everything."

"Lisa's really missing," Talli said desperately. "She needs help."

Sergeant Lansky pulled open the car door. "I'll go by Ms. Taylor's house and have a word with her parents, but I'm not filing any missing person report until she's been gone a full forty-eight hours. You be sure that's the only paper I have to file." He climbed into his car and slammed the door. With tires spinning up twin wakes of snow, the police car went sliding down the street and out of sight.

Talli stood beside the road, watching Sergeant Lansky vanish. Then she turned and looked at the faint silhouette of Volker's house through the curtains of falling snow. She

138

stomped back into her house on frozen feet and picked up the phone.

Thirty seconds later, Alex was on his way.

Talli would have liked to wait for him outside, but she had been in the cold too long already. She went up to check on her mother. The lights were still out in the bedroom, but Mrs. McAlister seemed to be sleeping normally. Again Talli wondered if she should call the doctor. If Volker really had drugged her mother, the hospital might be able to help. But after what had happened in the auditorium, Talli was more convinced than ever that whatever Volker was up to, it had nothing to do with drugs.

Talli heard Alex's car pulling into the driveway. Softly closing the bedroom door behind her, she hurried downstairs and pulled her coat from a kitchen chair. She slid into it as she ran out the door to meet Alex. He was still getting out of the Mustang when she reached him. "He's taken Lisa," she said.

"Who has?"

"Volker," Talli said. "She was waiting for me in my car, and now she's missing."

Alex pulled his padded coat from the seat of the car and shrugged it on. "Damn," he said. "How long has she been gone?"

"I don't know. At least an hour."

He looked around and kicked his foot at the snow. "And you're sure it was Volker?"

Talli grabbed his arm. "I'm positive. We've

139

got to do something right now!"

Alex stood for a moment looking down at the ground while the snow landed in his dark hair. Then he raised his head and looked at her with eyes that were two shades darker than normal. "I don't know what we can do," he said, "but let's go." He reached back into the car and pulled out a long metal flashlight. Without another word, he started for the gap between the houses. Talli was right behind him.

Snow fell from the fences and the low branches of trees as they passed. It spilled down the back of Talli's neck and melted into a freezing stream along her spine. In the tight space between the houses, the wind whipped the falling flakes into a blizzard. Talli held her hair back from her face with one hand, and held on to Alex with the other.

With the thick coating of white everywhere, it was hard to spot the board that opened into Volker's yard, and harder still to move it against the weight of drifted snow. Talli got down on her knees and squirmed through the opening, then held up the board so Alex could follow.

Volker's house was as dark as ever. Overhanging lips of snow hung from the edges of the roof, and more snow lined the wide windowsills. If there had been lights on, it might have looked like a Christmas postcard. In the dark, with its bare windows and unshoveled walks, it seemed only harsh and cold.

The backyard was a smooth, rolling blanket of snow. Only a few bony winter rosebushes marred the perfect surface. Alex started out across the yard, but Talli grabbed him. "The swimming pool," she whispered above the bitter wind. "It's under there somewhere. Stay to the left so we don't step on it."

Alex nodded and angled back to his left. Talli followed, stepping in his deep footprints and keeping her eyes on the dark house. They reached the back corner, the same place where they had stopped while running from the car on their previous visit. Talli glanced back across the yard. Even in the dim light, their footprints in the snow were a clear line of deep shadows. There would be no doubt that someone had come in here tonight, and no question of where they had come from.

Talli crouched down and looked through the basement window. The light was off, and she couldn't tell if anyone was there.

"What do we do now?" she asked.

Alex shrugged. "If you're serious about this," he said, "I guess we try to get inside."

"How?"

Alex turned and went up the flight of steps to the back porch. The screen door opened with a screech of dry hinges. Talli grimaced, but Alex held it open and grabbed the knob of the inner door. It rattled in his hand, but the door didn't open.

141

Talli came up the steps behind him. "Should we try the windows?"

"It's not worth it," Alex said. "Even if they're not locked, we'd probably have a hard time getting any of the ones in the basement open. They look like they've been painted over a dozen times. And unless you brought a ladder in your pocket, we'll never get in the others." He shook the door again, but it didn't move. "Maybe we can get in the front."

Talli examined the door. There was a small strip of window in the middle, through which she could make out a length of dark, bare hallway. The rest of the door was smooth wood. "Let me see your flashlight," she said.

Alex passed over the heavy tube. "I'd be careful about shining that inside," he said. "Someone might—"

Talli brought the butt of the flashlight down on the narrow window and smashed it into a million glittering pieces. She reached through the jagged opening and turned the knob on the other side. It opened with a solid click. As she pulled her hand out, a shard of glass tore the sleeve of Talli's jacket.

"We're in trouble now," Alex whispered weakly. They were both still for a long moment, waiting for a response from inside. No one shouted. Nothing moved.

"Come on," Talli said. "You were the one that said we needed to get in."

"I guess I was." He gestured toward the glass-littered hall. "Lead on."

Talli stepped inside. Her wet sneakers squeaked on the wood floor, and the crunch of broken glass was incredibly loud under her feet. She walked slowly, a step at a time. A door came up on the left. Talli peeked around the edge and into a spotless kitchen. More than spotless. Empty. Like the rest of the house, it looked as if it had been thoroughly cleaned and put away years before. Only a refrigerator, gently humming in a corner, gave any sign of life.

Alex came up behind her, and Talli jumped slightly as he touched her on the shoulder. "There must not be anybody here," he whispered. "If there was, they would have come down to see about the noise by now. Maybe they took Lisa someplace else."

"Let's check around," Talli said. She walked down the hallway, peeking around doorways into more empty rooms.

"Why don't we get out now?" suggested Alex. "Then we don't get caught, and we might be able to figure out where Lisa is."

Talli shook her head. "I'm not worried about getting caught; I just want to find her." She peeked around another door frame and found herself in the room they had seen from the outside. There was no furniture, only the cardboard box Talli had seen through the window.

143

She walked across the room, her every move echoing in the emptiness, and pulled up the top of the box. At first she couldn't make any sense of the contents. Then she saw it was clothing, a mixture of several types of clothing all jumbled together. There was men and women's clothing that ranged from a rumpled suit coat to a pair of high heels.

Alex came up and looked in. He reached into the box and pulled out a sheer negligee. "A girlfriend?"

Talli shook her head. "Look at the rest of this stuff. There's all different sizes in here." She took the gown from Alex's hand and stuffed it back into the box. "They couldn't all be from one person, or even one family."

"Does any of it—" started Alex. Then he shut his mouth quickly.

"Does any of it what?" Talli asked.

Alex looked away. "I was just going to ask if any of it looks like what Lisa was wearing."

Talli blinked at the implications of the question, but she turned back to the box and searched through the contents. "No," she said at last. "Nothing like Lisa's clothes here. Come on," she said. "Let's look in the basement."

Alex was slow to follow. "What's wrong?" Talli asked.

"It just hit me," he said.

"What?"

"Everything." He waved his hands around. "This house. The missing kids. Everything. If Volker is responsible, then he's probably . . . well, he could be some kind of serial killer."

Fifteen

❦

Serial killer? Talli thought in shock. She'd felt sure Volker was doing something terrible, but she had never put the words together, not even in her mind. *Serial killer.* It was a hard, evil phrase that brought an acid taste to Talli's mouth. "Let's find Lisa," she said.

They found the basement stairs behind a plain white door in the empty kitchen. Talli flipped the light switch, and the stairs were illuminated by a bare white bulb that dangled from a cord. The wooden staircase was steep, but wide. They went down it together.

The basement floor was concrete, with a scattering of faded rugs. Talli looked around, trying to orient herself. There were a few places that could have concealed a person. The first was a corner that was stacked with boxes. Alex walked over to it and glanced behind the stack. "Nothing here," he said.

"How about the boxes?" Talli asked.

He pulled open a box and looked in. "More clothes," he reported. "Looks like men's stuff."

The other suspicious spot was behind the tangle of vents and pipes near the furnace. There was some kind of bulky object there, something that looked perfect for holding one average-height eighteen-year-old girl.

Alex finished looking at the boxes and came up beside Talli. "It's a deep-freeze unit. The kind people usually keep meat in."

"I know," Talli said. She set the flashlight carefully on the concrete floor, then grabbed the handle of the freezer. She shoved, but the top stayed stubbornly closed. "Help me," she said to Alex.

"Do I have to?"

"The sooner we're done down here, the sooner we can go back," Talli said. She couldn't keep her voice from trembling. She had a bad feeling about the meat freezer. If anyone was inside, Talli knew they had to be dead from suffocation.

Alex grabbed the handle, and together they jerked the top open. The inside of the freezer was dark, stained, and smelly. It was also empty. The top swung shut with a thump.

"Can we go now?" Alex asked.

"As soon as we've looked upstairs." Talli

147

went back up the wooden steps to the kitchen. As soon as Alex reached the top, she flipped off the lights in the basement.

The staircase to the second floor was a bit narrower than the one leading to the basement. Alex went up a step ahead of Talli, holding his flashlight in his hand like a club.

The stairs groaned under Talli's feet. There was a noise behind her, and she turned so quickly that she almost fell from the steps. The front door was rattling in its frame, but it didn't open. *The wind*, she told herself, *it's only the wind*.

When she turned back, Alex was already at the top of the stairs and moving down the hall. She hurried to catch up. There were seven doors along the upstairs hallway, all of them closed. Alex walked to the first one on the right and turned the brass knob. The room was brightened by the light of a streetlamp outside. The yellow glow spilled over the heavy frame of a bed from which the mattresses had been removed.

"Do we look in the closet?" Alex asked.

Talli glanced at the dark door of the closet and shook her head. "Let's try the next room first. If we don't find anything, we can come back."

Alex shut the door while Talli opened the next one. This room was dark, and Alex had to switch on the flashlight to see inside. The circle of light showed another bed. This time, there were mattresses and sheets on the bed. There were other furnishings in the room, as well. A small table with a scattering of papers, and heavy drapes over the window.

"At least it's not all empty," Alex said. "This looks pretty normal."

Talli nodded, but as the light swung around the dark room, she had the distinct impression that something was wrong. "Let me see the flashlight," she said. Alex handed over the metal tube, and Talli slid the beam around the room again. She focused it for a moment on the ceiling, and passed it along the walls.

"There are no lights in here," she said.

"What?"

"No lights," Talli said. "No table lamp. No ceiling light. No floor lamp. No lights." She directed the light around the room as she spoke.

"Weird," Alex commented.

Talli switched off the flashlight. "Let's try the next room," she said, leading the way down the hallway. She reached for the knob of the next door, but Alex put his hand on her arm.

"Wait," he whispered.

Talli looked at him, baffled. "What is it?"

He nodded toward the floor. "Look there." Along the base of the door, in the thin crack between the door frame and the carpeted floor of the hallway, was a pale strip of light. "There may be someone inside," he said.

Talli reached for the knob again. "It may be

Lisa," she said, pulling the door open.

Talli was left squinting for a moment at the light from inside the room. After creeping through the dark house, her eyes weren't ready for the light of even a single lamp. When her sight cleared, she saw a large, four-poster bed with a bright red bedspread. There was a tall wooden chest on one side of the bed, and on the other a vanity table ringed by lights. In front of this table sat a woman.

She was a very old woman, with wild white hair and deep wrinkles cutting into skin as yellow-gray as factory smoke. A silky pink nightgown clung over her bony frame. She looked at Talli and Alex in confusion for a moment, then her blue eyes brightened.

"Hello," she said in a dry, rattling voice. "I didn't expect to see you here."

Talli tried to think of something to say, but her voice had deserted her. There was something about the woman. Something about her blue eyes that looked so familiar.

"We're sorry," Alex said. "We were just—"

"Breaking into someone's house," said a loud voice behind them.

Talli was vaguely aware of Alex turning and moving away from her side, but her eyes were still locked on the old woman. She heard something behind her, movement or blows, she couldn't tell.

Then she saw the reflection in the lighted

150

mirror of the vanity. In the mirror, the woman's hair was not white, but a deep golden blond. Her skin was not sallow, but pink and healthy. Her face was not thin and wrinkled, but smooth, young, and beautiful. It was Samantha Deveraux's face.

"Samantha?" Talli whispered in horror.

The woman's smile brightened, but before she could reply, the door swung closed with such force that it rattled in its frame. Talli stepped back, stunned. Without the light from the room, she was blind in the sudden darkness, and she had only an impression of movement before a heavy hand grabbed her shoulder.

The hand squeezed and lifted. For a moment Talli dangled from that grip like a mouse in the mouth of a cat, then her feet brushed against the carpet and she was dragged toward the top of the stairs. The hand relaxed its grip.

"Get downstairs," said a high reedy voice.

"I can't see," said Talli.

There was a click, and lights burst on along the hall and in the entry room. Talli swayed and almost fell as she looked down the steps. At the foot of the stairs stood Principal Volker.

She took a quick glimpse over her shoulder and saw Assistant Principal Lynch at her back with Alex at his side. Lynch was glaring down at Talli, while keeping one massive hand around Alex's arm. "Hurry up," he said.

Talli went down the steps on trembling legs.

Volker watched her approach with a slight smile on his thin face.

"Ms. McAlister," he said as she approached. "I must say that this is not entirely an unexpected visit."

"You thought I would come?"

"Yes," he said. "I quite expected you would." He glanced around the room. "I'm afraid that I have very little to offer you while we wait."

"Wait for what?" asked Alex. "What are you going to do to us?"

Volker turned away from them and stepped over to the front door. "I've already done all that I intend to," he said. Blue lights glared through the narrow window and brightened Volker's face.

"Ah, here comes Sergeant Lansky now."

"You called the police?" Talli asked in surprise.

"That's right," Lynch snarled. "Don't try to get away."

There was a rap at the door, and Volker swept it open to admit Sergeant Lansky. The policeman stepped around him with a nod and glared up at Talli. "You're in big trouble, McAlister. Don't think you're going to get off easy just because your father's on the force."

Volker laid a hand on the man's uniformed shoulder. "Please be calm," he said. "I don't want to cause any undue commotion."

Sergeant Lansky's glare was still fixed on

Talli. "These kids ought to be locked up," he said.

"There's no need for anything so harsh," Volker responded with a smile. "I know that Ms. McAlister is worried over her missing friend, and I assume Mr. Cole is here at her insistence."

"That's no excuse," said the sergeant. "I told her to stay out of trouble, and instead she came over here and broke in."

"I have some students coming by the school tomorrow to help clean and repair a few items," Volker said. "If these two were sentenced to help, I would drop any charge against them."

"Well—" started Sergeant Lansky.

"What about charges against him?" Talli blurted out. She pointed at Volker.

"Me?" Volker raised an eyebrow, and his smile grew wider. "Of what crime am I being accused?"

"Kidnapping."

"Kidnapping?" Volker's smile quickly turned into a frown. "I have seen nothing of your friend Ms. Taylor."

"I'm not talking about Lisa," Talli said. "I'm talking about Samantha Deveraux."

Now Volker's expression was one of complete confusion. "I'm aware that the child is missing," he said, "but I understood she was in some distant town."

Sergeant Lansky nodded. "We've had several phone calls."

Talli jerked her head toward the top of the stairs. "Samantha is right up there," she said.

The policeman looked at Volker. "What's she talking about?"

Volker spread his hands. "I assure you, Sergeant, I have no idea."

Talli turned to Alex. "You saw her," she said. "Tell them!"

Alex looked at her in confusion. "Saw Samantha? But Talli—"

"Tell me what you saw, son," Sergeant Lansky said.

Alex looked at policeman, then at Volker, then at Talli, then back at Sergeant Lansky. "I saw somebody," he said.

Sergeant Lansky took a half-step forward. "Was it the Deveraux girl?" he asked.

"No." Alex shook his head. "It was an old lady."

"Ah, that would be my mother," Volker said quickly. "She lives here with me."

Talli opened her mouth to protest. *I saw Samantha's face in the mirror*, she thought, but as she looked at the faces in front of her, she could imagine the kind of reaction that would get.

"I guess . . . I guess it was the lighting," she said weakly.

Sergeant Lansky snorted. "This girl's already fed me one cock-and-bull story tonight," he said to Volker.

Volker's good-natured smile was back. He

patted the officer on the back. "You can see that she's simply confused and worried over her friend. There's no need to carry this any further. As long as they're at school tomorrow," he said.

"I'll make sure that they are," said the policeman. He shook a beefy finger at Talli. "You two show up at school bright and early, or you'll be down at the station facing charges. You understand?"

"Yes, sir," Alex said promptly.

"I understand," Talli said.

"Good," said Principal Volker. His gray eyes met Talli's. Despite the smile on his lips, she found no warmth at all in his stare. "We'll take care of everything tomorrow," he said.

Sixteen

Saturday

The plowing crews had worked through the night, but the streets in Westerberg were still covered by a coat of ice. Talli looked out at the snow-covered sidewalks as Alex steered his car through the heart of town.

"I still can't believe we're actually going," she said.

"You want to end up in jail?" Alex asked.

"No, but I don't want to end up dead, either. Why won't you believe me?"

"About Samantha?" He shook his head vigorously. "Talli, that woman was *not* Samantha Deveraux. She must have been eighty years old. Maybe a hundred."

"It *was* Samantha. I saw her in the mirror."

Alex veered around a car that had gotten itself mired in the snow, and continued down the road. Talli looked over at him, waiting for his reply, but none came.

"Well," she said, "aren't you going to say anything?"

He shrugged. "What is there to say? It was an old woman. Lots of things were going on, and the light was strange. I can believe that you *thought* you saw something in the mirror, but I don't believe that woman was Samantha."

Talli gripped the car's vinyl dashboard and squeezed until her knuckles went white. "What about Lisa?" she asked through clenched teeth. "Volker said he knew I was upset about Lisa being missing, but nobody had told him about it. How did Volker know Lisa was missing?"

"Somebody must have told him," Alex replied. "He called the police to report us breaking in, maybe somebody told him about it then."

"What about all the other kids that are missing?"

Alex turned the car onto the road that ran past the school. Talli could feel the back tires slide in the snow. "I can believe that Volker is behind it," Alex said, "and when your dad gets back tonight, I'll stand right beside you and back you up on everything I can. But there's a long way from saying that Volker snatched some kids to saying he can make someone get eighty years older in a week." He shook his head. "It's the difference between reality and fantasy."

He pulled off the road and bumped over a snow drift as he turned into the parking lot. There were a few cars in the lot, no more than half a dozen. The yellow lines that usually divided the parking spaces were hidden under the snow. Alex pulled his Mustang up next to the school and killed the engine. "Let's go," he said.

Talli wanted to scream, or to cry. If Alex hadn't been going, she would have happily sat at home until Sergeant Lansky came to throw her into a holding cell. Explaining to her father why she was under arrest was not nearly as frightening as going in to see Volker. But Alex was going, and Talli wasn't about to let him go alone.

The air was bitterly cold when she stepped out of the car. The sky had cleared during the night, bringing an end to the snow, but the temperature had continued to drop. Now the sky was an ashen winter blue, and the sun seemed shrunken and pale. Talli crossed the strip of snow-encrusted sidewalk as quickly as she could, and shoved open the metal door at the front of the school. There was a pool of light near the doors. Beyond that, the hallways were almost as dark as when Talli had sneaked in the night before. Being back at school made her uneasy. The sound of the thing that had chased her through the auditorium played itself back in her mind so clearly that she shuddered.

Alex came up behind her. "I guess we're supposed to go to the office," he said.

He started off into the darkness. Talli watched him moving in and out of the dim emergency lights. He was almost at the office before she swallowed hard and started after him.

Volker greeted them at the door to the outer office. "Good morning, my friends," he said. "I'm glad you decided to show up today."

Talli wanted to tell him that they were *not* friends, but she bit back the words and followed Alex into the office. There was no secretary for this special Saturday audience with Volker. If there were other students around, they were already off somewhere else in the school. Volker led them into his office, closed the door softly, and sat behind his desk.

"Please," he said. "Take a seat." He gestured toward the two chairs that faced his desk.

"What do you want us to do?" Talli asked.

Volker drummed his long fingers on the bare metal top of the desk. "There will be no more pretense between us, Ms. McAlister." He lifted his hands from the desk and circled one finger around another. "We two have been sparring in the dark. From now on, we will deal with each other face-to-face."

"What are you talking about?" Talli asked, but she was only stalling. She knew well enough what Volker meant. They had been enemies from the first moment he had come out of the darkness behind the stage. He might have been saving her from some boys and their knives, but that didn't make them any less enemies.

"Tsk, tsk." The sound was reproachful and sarcastic. "Perhaps this will not be as civilized as I had hoped."

"I don't understand," Alex said. "What's going on?"

"Perhaps you don't, Mr. Cole," Volker said, "but she understands me. She understands me very well."

Talli leaned forward in her chair. "Why are you here?" she demanded.

Volker's smile broadened. "That's more like it." He leaned back in his chair and folded his hands behind his head. "I'm here," he said, "because I felt that this was an opportunity. Small town, troubled school . . . it seemed to demand someone of my background."

"Background?"

"Would it surprise you to know that I have been employed in a similar position before?" he asked. "In those days I was called headmaster instead of principal, but the duties are much the same."

"How long ago was that?" Talli asked.

"Oh, not too terribly long. Perhaps one or two centuries?"

Alex jumped to his feet. Talli looked over and saw that his face was very pale. "You were right, Talli. This guy is crazy. Let's get out of here."

160

Volker's smile disappeared in an instant. "Sit down, Mr. Cole."

"I—" Alex began.

There was a flash, a whirl of movement too rapid to follow. Alex's head snapped back. A thin trickle of blood dripped from the corner of his mouth. Volker stood over him with one long hand tangled in the collar of Alex's coat. "Sit," he said. His voice was soft, but there was no doubt that it was a command, not a request.

Alex sat. His eyes were glazed and dull. His mouth hung open in dumb surrender.

The whole thing had happened so fast, Talli had barely had time to blink. When she turned her head, Volker was back behind his desk, smiling and relaxed.

"What did you do to him?" she asked.

"Most people are much more susceptible to my . . . talents than are you, Ms. McAlister. Your young friend here is particularly malleable."

A new emotion swelled up from Talli's stomach, replacing the fear that had filled her. It came burning into her throat like acid. It was anger, the purity of which was tainted only by hatred. "You didn't come to help the school," she snarled at Volker. "Why are you here?"

"You're right, of course." Volker's voice was as soft and calm as ever. "The school's problems only provided me with a convenient cover to which I was well suited. I came here for the same purpose that I come to all places—to feed."

"I know what you are," Talli said.

"Do you?" Volker leaned toward her over the desk. "I'd dearly love to hear that."

"You're a vampire," she said, and then she screamed.

Volker's features were running like dripping candle wax. As Talli scrambled to her feet, knocking over her folding chair in the process, the flesh of Volker's narrow face flowed and rippled. A black stain appeared at the roots of his hair and rose quickly. In moments, his appearance was completely transformed, made over into a face Talli knew well from dozens of horror films.

"Good evening," said the thing with Dracula's face. "I vant to drink your blood. Blah. Blah." He opened his mouth to reveal fangs as long as a rattler's, then he began to laugh.

Talli turned to Alex. She pulled on his arm, but it dropped back to his side, limp. "Come on," she whispered, while Volker's laughter filled the room. "Come on!"

"Ms. McAlister," said a voice at her back.

Talli found that she was trembling from head to foot. The muscles in her neck seemed to have frozen, letting her turn her head only in a slow, unsteady series of jerks. The anger that had been a fire in her guts only a moment before was gone, washed away by white-cold terror.

The figure at Volker's desk still wore the same pale gray suit, but it bore no resemblance to Volker. The face was young, no older than Talli. Young and very handsome, with wavy hair so black it was almost blue, and startling bright green eyes in a broad square-cut face. "I'm sorry," he said in a pleasant voice. "I'm afraid I let my manners slip quite badly. I never intended to frighten you."

Oh, yes you did, Talli thought. *You meant to scare me good. And you did.*

The young man in Volker's suit gestured at the chair, which had somehow righted itself. "Won't you please return to your seat? I have more to discuss with you."

Talli sank back into the seat, grateful to be off legs that felt as weak as wet paper. She wanted to ask something else, but the terror inside had its own question—the only one that mattered. "Are you going to kill me?" she asked.

Seventeen

The young man's handsome face settled into a look of great concern. "There are basically three types of people," he said. "Some are very open to my talents. Perhaps even capable of acquiring my abilities for themselves. I'm always looking for people like this, Ms. McAlister. Always. There are a second group of people. People that are regrettably good for little but the modicum of sustenance they can provide me."

"You mean you eat them," interrupted Talli.

The young man waved a hand and wrinkled his nose, as if he found the very idea distasteful. "Nothing so crude as that," he said. "In many cases, I take what I need from them with very little harm. Only those who are most sensitive are at risk."

"Like Samantha Deveraux?"

"A tragic case," he replied. "Truly tragic." His mask of concern slipped, and his lips parted in a smile full of smooth, white movie-star teeth. "She has provided a great deal of energy, though."

"You're a monster," Talli said in a hoarse whisper.

"I don't deny it. You called me a vampire," he said, "and I think you are right. At least, the legend that you call vampire probably originated with someone like me. Werewolves, as well. Just think. If it wasn't for people like me, many of those horror books you like so much would never have been written."

"How do you know I like horror books?" Talli asked. She wasn't sure she cared about the answer, but a part of her brain was still floating above the flood of terror, and that part of her brain was telling her to Keep Volker Talking. If she kept him talking long enough, perhaps she would think of a way that both she and Alex could escape.

"I am learning much about you at this moment," he said. He gestured toward Alex. "Your friend is very open to me, and he knows you quite well."

"You can read minds," Talli said.

"Only of those who are open to me," said the young man. "And I can do other mental tricks as well. I assume it was you that triggered the little trap I left here at the school?"

"That thing in the auditorium . . ."

"Amusing, wasn't it? A little something I left for anyone who might get too curious." He smiled. "As long as we're having this heart-to-heart, is there anything else you want to know?"

"You can change shapes," Talli said.

"That much should be obvious," said the young man.

"That's why you have all those boxes of clothes. So you can be anybody you want."

"Correct."

"You're not really very much like vampires in the movies. You don't drink blood."

"No. I sometimes even drink . . . wine," he said. This remark caused another horrible bout of laughter.

"But you don't like light," Talli said when he was done.

"I'm not very much like movie vampires." The young man leaned back, folding his hands behind his head in the same way that the elder Volker had done minutes before. "I share few of their weaknesses. In truth, light is of little bother to those who have been blessed with this gift for as long as I. But it often fells those who have been empowered for only a short time. You really are very astute, Ms. McAlister. I knew I was right about you."

"Right about what?" Talli asked. She glanced around the room without moving her head, looking for anything that might double as a weapon. Beside her, Alex continued to stare without blinking.

"I said there were three groups of people," said the young man. "There are those that are open to me, those that feed me, and there are those like you. People who are closed to me."

There was a letter opener on top of the file cabinet. Talli didn't remember seeing it the night before, but there was no mistaking it now. *Would it hurt him?* she wondered. *If I stabbed him with it, would he even bleed?*

"You have a great strength," the young man continued. "It may be that which protects you. Those people who are open to me—like your friend here—can come to partake of the gift that I possess. But they are generally weak and foolish. They may gain the abilities, but they will never fully appreciate them. In the past I have found that it's people like you—a rare group—who can come to thoroughly know the powers I now possess." He unfolded his hands and leaned toward her. "Lynch was one such as you. Weeks were spent before I brought him over to me. I myself was closed to the one who made me what I am."

"You were human, then?" Talli asked. She put her weight on one foot, preparing to jump for the letter opener.

"I was once," he said, "but I'm more than that now."

"And you want to make me what you are?"

"Yes," he said. "You will find that—"

There was a knock at the door. The young man's face melted and thinned. The dark hair grew grayer and shorter. In a moment the figure in the chair was again Principal Volker.

"I'm busy at the moment," he called in Volker's voice.

The door cracked open, and Sergeant Lansky stuck his balding head in. "I wanted to make sure that these two showed up," he said, jerking his head toward Talli and Alex.

"Thank you, Sergeant," Volker said. "I appreciate your diligence."

In the light that spilled in through the open door, Talli saw something sparkling in Alex's fingers. She reached over and unfolded his limp hand, pulling out the keys to his Mustang.

"You're sure this is how you want to handle it?" Sergeant Lansky asked.

"Quite sure," Volker said. "They'll get a suitable punishment from me."

Talli sprang from her chair and pushed past Sergeant Lansky. His shout rang in her ears as she sprinted down the hall. She had seen how fast Volker could move, and she had no illusion that she could outrun him. But perhaps Sergeant Lansky would get in his way. Or maybe Volker wouldn't want to reveal himself in front of the policeman. In any case, Talli doubted she would get a better chance.

She heard heavy steps pounding along the

hall behind her as she reached the doors and pushed her way out into the pale winter sunshine. The light reflecting off the snow was blinding, but Talli charged on, her feet slipping on the icy ground as she tried to make out Alex's car in a world full of glare.

She found the Mustang, yanked open the door, and slid in. Out of the corner of her eye, she saw Sergeant Lansky run from the school as she stuck Alex's key into the ignition. The policeman spotted her and began to run for the car as she ground the motor into life. He reached the side of the Mustang, but Talli slapped the door lock into place.

In her rearview mirror, she saw Volker standing at the door of the school. He stood under the awning, at the border between shadow and light. Talli had a sudden memory of how haggard Volker had looked that sunny morning she and Lisa had seen him coming into school. She had an idea that sunlight bothered him a great deal more than he had admitted.

A fist thumped the window beside her face. Talli jerked around and saw Sergeant Lansky still clinging to the door. "Open up!" he shouted. "Police!"

Talli gunned the engine. The car spun for a moment on the ice, then spurted forward. Sergeant Lansky held on for a second longer, then dropped away. She caught a brief glimpse of him tumbling through the snow.

The Mustang bounced up onto the highway, fishtailing badly on the slick surface. A car coming the other way skidded past with a blare of horns as Talli fought to get the vehicle under control. At last it straightened out, and she rolled up the road as fast as she dared, leaving the school behind.

Alex, said a voice in her mind. *You left Alex behind. What about Alex?*

"I can't help him if I'm dead," Talli said aloud. She slowed the car to a stop at an intersection and looked left and right. Getting the keys and getting out of the school had seemed like a great idea at the time. Now that she had done it, she had absolutely no idea what to do next.

A glance in the rearview mirror showed a dark car fishtailing up the road behind her. Talli hit the gas again, turning right for no particular reason. She was only fifty feet from the intersection when the other car came skidding through and turned after her. Talli couldn't make out the form hunched over the wheel, but she assumed it was either Volker or the sergeant. She pressed the gas pedal as far as she dared, and went speeding down the road that led away from Westerberg to the east.

The dark car stayed with her as Talli swept down a hill, up another, and around a turn where the rear end of the Mustang went into a spin. The steering wheel twisted and jumped in her hands, and she had to fight to get it straightened out before sliding into the next turn.

When she looked back, the dark car had lost some ground, but it was still behind her. Talli bit her lip, trying to think of the road ahead. How could she get away from the dark car? She hit a straight stretch, and pressed the gas pedal all the way to the floor board. Even without curves, the Mustang fishtailed back and forth as Talli picked up speed.

She looked in the mirror and saw that she had put a good gap between herself and the dark car. There was a building coming up on the right. It was a big whitewashed garage that had been out of business for years, but was still surrounded by the snow-covered wrecks of a dozen old cars.

A hideout, Talli thought. *If I can only get behind that building* . . . She slammed on the brakes.

The car went into a spin. Talli clung to the steering wheel as the world spun around her. For what seemed like an hour, she was traveling backward down the highway. Then the Mustang snapped around again. The tires along the right side skated off the blacktop. There was a sharp thump, and Talli saw a mailbox go flying away from the fender. The wheels actually left the ground for a moment.

Another half-turn, and the car slid sideways into the parking lot of the long-closed service station. A shudder went through it as the tires struck the concrete base that had once held the gas pumps. The blow knocked it into another spin. The world blurred around Talli again.

She wasn't sure when it stopped. Her head kept reeling for long moments after it seemed that the Mustang had ceased to move. Talli barely had time to pry her trembling hands from the steering wheel before the other car came sweeping toward her down the road.

Jail, she thought. *That doesn't sound so bad. I have to make sure that it's Sergeant Lansky that gets me, and that he takes me to jail instead of back to Volker.*

The dark car came closer, drew even, and went past without slowing. She watched it drive around the next curve and disappear behind a grove of snow-covered trees.

"It wasn't after me," she whispered. A burst of hysterical laughter escaped through her teeth, but she bit it off. She squeezed her eyes shut, ignoring the tears that leaked down her face. Then she took a deep breath, opened her eyes, and reached out to adjust the rearview mirror.

Assistant Principal Lynch's face grinned at her from the mirror. A hand reached over the seat and pushed her to the side with such force that the breath was knocked from her lungs.

Lynch squeezed his heavy frame through the gap between the seats. "Some ride," he said as he climbed behind the steering wheel. "Now let's go home."

Eighteen

The gate opened slowly. Talli watched the metal bars slide away, revealing the front of Volker's house. The house she'd broken into only the night before. It was the first time in years that she'd had a clear look at the house in daylight. It was rather pretty, with its tall windows and steeply sloping roof. The prettiness did nothing to cheer Talli.

Lynch steered Alex's car through the open gate and pulled it to the side of the house. "Get out," he said, "and don't think about running."

Talli got out, but she *did* think about running. She wondered if Lynch knew about the loose board in the back fence. She wondered if he was as fast as Volker.

His thick fingers wrapped around her arm while she was still thinking, and he dragged her toward the front door with brutal force. At the steps, Lynch didn't bother to let her walk—he hoisted her off her feet and carried her up with her boots dangling above the ground. He opened the door while Talli rubbed her wrenched shoulder. Lynch shoved her inside, stepped in behind her, and slammed the front door.

He glared at her from his deep-set eyes. "I'd like to take you now," he said. "I'd like to drink you dry and throw away the husk."

Talli's mouth felt as dry as dust. She licked her lips before replying. "But you won't," she said. "Volker wants me for himself."

Lynch's face extended into a snout, became a muzzle lined with jagged teeth. "Don't get cocky, little girl," he snarled. "The big bad wolf might eat you yet."

Talli tried to turn away, but Lynch grabbed her with hands that had grown wide and furry. "You won't hurt me," she said. "Volker would be mad."

"Accidents happen," growled Lynch. A drop of saliva dripped from his muzzle and fell on Talli's upturned face. His paw slipped around behind her back and snagged onto her coat. He pulled her like a rag doll to the stairs. "Will you climb yourself, or do I throw you?" he asked.

"I'll climb," she said. Lynch relaxed his grip on her clothing, and Talli turned to the staircase and began to climb. Behind her the boards creaked under Lynch's weight. Talli remembered something she'd read once about the gallows where they used to hang people. There were thirteen steps up to the platform of a gallows. She thought that the people who had climbed those thirteen steps had probably felt the way she felt as she climbed to the upper floor of Volker's house.

She reached the top and started to turn around. Lynch shoved her from behind. "Keep going," he said.

Talli walked down the hallway. The seven doors were still closed. Talli stared at the third door on the right, the door to the room where Samantha had been the night before. Was she still there? Still sitting in front of her vanity, smiling at a reflection that was no longer hers?

"Stop," Lynch said.

Talli stopped. Lynch moved past her and opened the door to the first room. She was relieved to see that Lynch's face was back to normal, though she doubted it meant she was any safer. Inside the room was the same unfilled bed frame that she had seen the night before. With daylight coming through the window, she could see that the wallpaper was an attractive pattern of tiny roses on a background of pale yellow. This had probably been a happy place . . . once.

"Get in the closet," Lynch said.

"What?"

"There are no locks on these bedroom doors,

and I'm not going to waste my time watching you. You'll have to wait in the closet till he gets here."

Talli looked across the room at the dark wooden door of the closet. "I'm not going in there," she said. The words were hardly out of her mouth before she was flying over the bed frame. She hit the wall with such force that plaster dust sifted down from the ceiling.

Lynch leaned over her, his face rippling like a flag in the wind. "First accident," he said. "You do what I tell you, understand? You wouldn't want another accident, would you?"

Talli shook her head. Lynch lifted her from the ground and carried her over to the closet. He pulled the door open with one hand and shoved her inside with the other. "Don't give me any reason to come back up here before he comes," Lynch said. "The next accident might be fatal."

The door slammed, leaving Talli in total darkness. She heard the knob turn, heard the tumblers click as the lock engaged. Then came the creaking of boards as Lynch stalked back across the room. The noises faded into the distance as he went down the stairs. Then the only sound was her own breathing.

She wondered how long it would take Volker to arrive. She didn't think it would be too long. Whatever he was doing, she suspected he was anxious to take care of her.

176

Lynch was one such as you. The words played back in her head. Volker wanted to make her a monster like him. She shivered in the dark. Was she the only one that he had made this offer to, or had some of the missing students become things like him? She didn't know. She only knew that she didn't want to be in this closet when Volker arrived.

Talli ran her hands over the walls of her narrow prison. Her fingers found only bare wood. She tried the doorknob, but it wouldn't turn. She thought about trying to break the door down, but the wood was thick and Talli was no linebacker. Besides, even if it worked, Lynch was sure to hear.

She reached over her head and felt the metal bar that had been used to hang clothes from. It would be a good weapon if she could get it loose. Above that she felt the bottom of a shelf.

"What's up there?" Talli whispered, taking comfort in the sound of her own voice. She gripped the metal bar and pulled herself up until she could get one foot on the doorknob. From there she wiggled through the gap between the front of the shelf and the door.

The shelf was bare. She slid her hands over the wood, feeling nothing but dust. Twisting around, she started to climb back to the lower part of the closet. Then her head hit the ceiling. And the ceiling moved.

Talli reached up and pushed. A panel slid

aside, and faint blue light washed into the closet. Talli worked her way up, and got her head through the square opening. Rafters stretched out in front of her as far as she could see. Light came in through distant slat-covered windows. She had found her way into the attic.

Talli pushed against the closet door with her boots, working her way onto the shelf, through the gap, and into the attic. She found the panel that she had moved and put it back in place, hoping it would take them a while to figure out how she had escaped.

She walked across the attic, stepping only on the rafters. There were several trapdoors like the one she had come through, but she avoided them. The idea of going back down into the house didn't seem very attractive.

She went first to the window, hoping to make her escape from there, but the window did not open. In fact, it didn't look as if it had ever been designed to open. Even if it had, there was nothing under it but a thirty-foot drop to the snowy ground. There were a few items stacked near the window. Talli suspected they were left-overs from the former tenants. A large aquarium with a crack across one side sat dry in the corner. Beside it was a shabby broom and a large wooden trunk. Talli opened the trunk. There seemed to be nothing inside but moth-eaten clothing, but when Talli dug down a little, she touched the cool metal top of a smaller box. She found a handle on it and pulled it up through the old clothes.

Even in the dim light, there was no mistaking the form of the red metal box. It was a toolbox. She opened the top and found the tools inside to be nothing more than a few rusted bolts and a hammer with a handle held together by tape. "I can see why they left this behind," Talli said. She lifted the hammer out of the box and swung it around. It felt good in her hand. She had no idea if it would be of any use, but the idea of having some weapon, any weapon, made her feel better.

She took the broom, put her foot over the end, and twisted it to the side. The wood splintered with a dry crack, and the straw-covered end dropped off, leaving a jagged point behind.

With wooden spear in one hand and hammer in the other, Talli walked over to the nearest trapdoor and shoved it open with her foot. She looked down into the darkness below. She didn't know which closet this door opened into—it could lead her straight to Lynch.

If I stay here, they'll catch me for sure, Talli thought. She put her feet through the opening and eased herself down into the darkness.

The closet she dropped into was identical to the one she had left. There was the same shelf, and the same narrow gap between it and the door. She dropped the broom as she tried to get down, and it clattered against the wooden door.

Talli froze, holding her breath, but she didn't hear anything. After a few seconds, she went on.

She eased herself down to the bottom of the closet and waited until her breathing had settled before putting her hand to the knob. It turned easily, and bright light spilled in as she slowly opened the door. She recognized the room as soon as she saw the bright red bed. It was the room where she'd seen Samantha.

Talli thought about climbing back up. She wasn't frightened of Samantha in the way that she was frightened of Lynch or Volker. She just didn't want to see her. She wasn't sure she could stand to see again what Volker had done to her.

Still, it was better to face Samantha than to take the risk of dropping in on Lynch, and every second of waiting was a second in which Volker might show up to claim her. Talli reached down to pick up the broom handle from the floor. The fingers of her other hand gripped the hammer tightly. She stepped out into the room.

Samantha's face was still in the mirror. Bright, beautiful, and faintly smiling. Wild white hair prevented Talli from seeing anything of the figure in the chair. As quietly as she could, she began to creep across the room toward the door.

In the mirror, Samantha's blue eyes turned toward Talli. "Tallibeth," she said.

Talli froze at the sound of her voice. It was not a human voice. It was more like the sound of wind in a dusty cave. The figure in front of the mirror slowly turned. With every movement it made, Talli's need to scream grew, but her throat was too tight to scream, too tight to even breathe.

The thing that had been Samantha Deveraux looked at her. It was no longer an old woman. It was a skeleton encased in parchment hide so thin that every bone was visible. The lips had peeled away to reveal long rows of yellowed teeth, and all that remained of the nose was a pair of gaping holes. In the middle of that dry brown skull, Samantha's eyes rolled in sockets from which the flesh had curled back. "I'm so glad to see you," said the thing.

Talli staggered backward. The hammer dropped from her hand and thudded against the floor. The broom handle went rattling down beside it. She worked her mouth, trying to say something, anything.

The skeleton thing rose from its chair with a sound like the movement of rusty hinges. The silky nightgown draped over bare ribs and clung to the jutting bones of the thing's hips. "Did he promise you, too?" the thing asked in its dusty voice.

"Promise me?" choked Talli.

It nodded, an action that made its neck bones rattle like dice. "To be beautiful," it said. It lifted the ivory brush it held in one hand and pulled it slowly through the white hair. A hank of hair pulled away from the head, bringing with it a patch of dry scalp. Pale bone showed through the gap. "Beautiful forever," the thing crooned. There was no expression on its face. There was nothing to even have an expression *with*. But Talli could have sworn that it was smiling.

Black spots swam at the edge of Talli's vision. She wanted to close her eyes until she felt better. More than that, she wanted to lie down and sleep until all of this nightmare just went away.

The bony thing took another creaking step toward her. "Are you here to stay with me?" it asked.

Talli turned and ran.

Before she could reach the door, it exploded off its hinges. It flew across the room and went spinning past the skeleton Samantha. Talli had a momentary glimpse of blue eyes turning in their raw sockets to watch the door go past.

Then Lynch was in front of her. He put his huge hand around her throat and lifted her from her feet. Talli pried at his fingers, pounded at his arm with her fists. She might as well have been striking stone. He put his wide face very close to hers. "I told you to stay put," he growled. "Now I suppose we'll have to arrange that accident." He began to squeeze.

Lynch said something more, or at least his mouth kept moving, but whatever he said was lost in the ringing in Talli's ears. He shook her from side to side, and she could feel her legs swinging like a puppet with its strings cut. Her arms got heavy, and the effort of pounding at Lynch's hands grew until she could do nothing but let her arms dangle uselessly at her sides. Blackness was coming up to claim her.

Then stars burst in her skull and pain swept over her. It took her a moment to realize that Lynch had thrown her across the room. She sat up, sparks still filling her vision.

"This is your last chance," he said. "You're going back in the closet, and if you move an inch, I'm going to bite your head off. You understand that?"

The skeleton thing moved to him and touched him with a bony hand. "Are you going to hurt her?" it asked.

Lynch looked at it in disgust. "Get away from me," he said. He gave the skeleton thing a push, and it tumbled back onto the red bed with a sound like children's blocks being kicked over.

Talli got to her knees and picked up the broom handle. "Stay away from me," she said. Her voice trembled more than she would have liked. "Just stay back."

"Put that down," Lynch said.

"Stay back," Talli repeated.

Lynch stepped forward. He was fast, maybe as fast as Volker. His hand cut through the air like a scythe, snapping the broomstick off in her hands, leaving her with a piece of wood no more than a foot long. He stood over her. "Get up and come with me," he snarled.

Talli took the piece of wood in her hands and slashed upward. The sharp point cut through Lynch's shirt. As tough as he had seemed to Talli's hands, the wood went into him as if he were made of jelly, going deep into the notch between his ribs.

Lynch stepped back. There was a look on his face that might have been surprise. He grabbed the end of the wooden stake and pulled on it. It came about halfway out. He grunted and pulled again, but the wood didn't move. "You little fool," he said in his high reedy voice.

Talli found the hammer on the floor. Gripping it with both hands, she swung it with all her might. Her first blow struck Lynch in the hand. A finger snapped off and fell to the floor, dancing there like a fish out of water.

She swung again, hitting the end of the stake and driving it back under his ribs. Lynch grunted again. He put both hands over the place where the stake had gone in. Something began to pour out between his fingers, something that was thick and black and definitely not human blood. He fell.

Talli swung the hammer again, striking his hands, and bringing a surge of the black fluid. Bile stung Talli's throat as she lifted the hammer for another swing.

Lynch rolled over and began to crawl toward

the door, leaving an oily trail in his wake. Talli saw the point of the wood sticking though his back. She swung at it and missed. The hammer buried itself in Lynch's back.

Lynch screamed. Talli jumped as he buckled and reached back, trying to pull out the hammer. The flesh on his head and arms twitched as if he had a nest of eels under his skin. He got one hand under him and turned to look at Talli. His face was dissolving, dripping away from the bone. The arm that held him up snapped in half, and he fell back. His other hand made a few more weak attempts to claw at his back, then he was still.

Black and yellow fluid seeped from the sleeves of his shirt, from the ends of his pants, from the holes that the hammer and stake had made. In a matter of seconds, there was only a heap of clothing floating in a pool of foul-smelling muck. The hammer fell from the bundle of empty clothing and thumped on the floor.

Talli was sobbing, each breath aching in her lungs. She climbed to her feet and stepped back against the wall, trying to stay out of the goo.

"Tallibeth," said a voice at the door.

Talli turned, ready to face Volker. But instead she found herself looking into the brown eyes of Lisa Taylor.

Nineteen

❦

"Lisa!" Talli cried. She staggered toward her friend, stepping through the pool of goo that had until moments before been Assistant Principal Lynch.

Lisa opened her arms and pulled Talli close. "It's all right now," she whispered. "Everything's all right."

Talli stared at her friend. She was wearing the same baggy sweater that she'd been in when Talli last saw her. Her hair was a mess and she seemed a little worn, but she looked basically all right. In all the madness, Lisa was a strand of sanity.

Talli buried her face in Lisa's brown hair for a moment as she tried to hold in her sobs. She gave Lisa a final hug and pulled away. "Where have you been?" she asked.

"Right here," whispered Lisa. "They've been keeping me here."

"We came looking for you," Talli said. She wiped her eyes with the back of her hand, dabbing away the tears. "Alex and I came looking for you."

"I know. It's okay."

"And then the police came, and Alex . . . Oh, God. I left Alex with Volker." Talli started for the door, but Lisa blocked her way.

"I'm sure he's okay too," she whispered. Lisa stepped into the room, moving stiffly. She looked at the pile of bones on the bed. "Is that what's left of the girl?"

"What?"

Lisa shook her head. "She sure went downhill fast." Her voice was not a whisper this time, but it was strange and hoarse.

"Lisa," Talli said, "are you okay?"

"Dandy," Lisa replied. "Never been better." She turned toward Talli with a bright smile. "Fooled you, didn't I?"

Talli's heart dropped into her stomach. "Volker," she whispered.

"Nope," said the brown-eyed girl. The hair on her head straightened and became straw-yellow, her eyes lightened, and her face lengthened.

"Pretty damn good, huh?" Morris South asked. "Haven't figured out how to walk yet, though. And voices—man, are voices hard to do. But you give me another day to practice, and

I'll fool her mother." There was a snapping and popping as muscle and bone shifted on his frame. Lisa's sweater stretched as his shoulders widened.

Talli backed away, moving toward the hammer and piece of broken wood that still lay among the pile of clothes where Lynch had died. "Where is Lisa?" she asked.

"Gone," Morris said. He took a step toward her. "Gone, gone, gone. Just another midnight snack." He made a sound like someone slurping a milk shake through a straw.

Talli bent and reached for the hammer. His hand closed on her wrist, and he yanked her back to her feet. His face twisted, and his hair turned the color of flame. In seconds, Talli was looking into a copy of her own face. "Volker let me finish off your friend," said the mirror image. "He's been very, very good to me. Maybe he'll let me have you, too." He shrank inside the sweater, becoming the same size as Talli. Then he released her hand and pirouetted around with one hand on top of his newly red hair.

"I think I could do you," he said. "What do you think? Am I Tallibeth McAlister, all-around good girl?" He smiled with her teeth.

Talli could feel gooseflesh marching up her arms. She took another step back and stumbled over the vanity seat. She grabbed it quickly and held it up in front of her. "You won't fool anyone," she said.

"Don't be so sure," said the counterfeit Talli. "Come closer, so I can compare."

Talli stepped back. Morris charged. Talli swung the chair, but he was too fast. He ducked under her blow, knocked the chair from her hands, and came up right in her face. His imitation Talli hands took her by the shoulders, holding her with a strength that the real Talli could never match.

"Hiya, sis," he whispered.

The chair he had thrown struck the window and crashed through. The blinds and drapes collapsed in a heap. Talli had a glimpse of the snow-covered landscape and the steeply sloping roof under the window as orange afternoon light came pouring in. A pool of brightness surrounded Morris and Talli.

Morris blinked and released her shoulders. He stepped back, looking at his hands. With a crackle like burning newspaper, small fires appeared on his hands, on his face, in his hair.

"Bummer," he said solemnly. Then the fire crackled up in earnest, pouring out of the collar of the sweater, swirling around, consuming him in a pillar of flame that reached to the ceiling.

When the fire died, there was nothing more than a scorched spot on the carpet to mark the spot where Morris had stood.

There was a slow, measured clapping from the hallway, and Volker stepped into the room. Talli looked at him and laughed. It was not the

189

hysterical gales that had threatened her a few minutes before, it was the laughter of someone who was too tired to be afraid. "It's about time," she said.

"My congratulations," Volker said. His face was basically the same as the one he had worn in public, but he seemed younger and more relaxed. He leaned against the frame from which Lynch had torn the door. "You've dispatched two of my companions quite quickly," he said. "Mr. South was very young, but Mr. Lynch had been with me for years. I'm quite impressed."

"You may not be a movie vampire," Talli said, "but you can die like one."

"I think you'll find that sunlight is not as effective on me as it is on novices," he replied. "I will admit that having large objects driven through my body would be quite unpleasant." He nodded toward the place where Lynch had fallen. "But then, I think you'd find having a broomstick through your chest just as disagreeable."

"What about crosses? Holy water? That kind of thing."

Volker smiled and pushed himself upright. "If you'll excuse me, I don't think I'll stand here and give you a list of ways I might die." He took a step toward her, his feet squishing in the muck left behind by Lynch's death. "Not that I expect you to have a chance to take advantage of any of this knowledge."

There was a clattering sound from the bed. Volker stopped as the skeleton form of Samantha Deveraux rose from the sheets. With bony fingers, it smoothed the gown over its cadaverous frame. "Henry," it said. "I'm glad you're home."

Volker looked at it with no apparent emotion. "Good afternoon, my dear," he said.

The skeleton moved toward him, put its hands on the lapels of his jacket, and placed its ghastly face close to his. "You shouldn't leave me alone so long. That terrible Mr. Lynch, he tried to hurt me."

Volker took the bony hands between his fingers and lifted them away from his jacket. "Mr. Lynch won't be bothering you anymore, my dear."

Talli looked around the room. The hammer was two steps away. The stake was still lost in Lynch's clothing. Volker's eyes seemed locked on the ghastly remains of Samantha. Talli took a half-step toward the hammer.

Volker reached out and caressed Samantha's parchment cheek. "You know, my dear, it has been a pleasure having you as a guest this week," he said.

"I'm glad," murmured the skeleton in its desert of a voice. "This is only the beginning."

Talli took another step. The hammer was right under her hand. She bent slowly.

"No," Volker said. "I'm afraid it's the end. I have derived all the energy I can from your condition, and maintaining this illusion is now a losing proposition." He took his hand from the thing's cheek and passed it over the lolling eyes.

"What do you mean?" it asked. "I—" The dry voice stopped, and the skeleton bent its head. It raised a wasted hand and looked at the bony fingers. A shudder ran through it with a rattle like castanets. Slowly it ran the hand over its face, feeling the lipless mouth, the gaping holes where the nose had been, the fleshless void around the eyes.

The mouth opened, and it made the most terrible sound that Talli had ever heard. A screeching cry that went on and on, climbing up the scale on a torrent of pure horror.

Volker struck it a casual, backhanded blow, and the whole thing flew apart. Sundered bones rattled off the walls. The skull came to rest at Talli's feet just as her hand closed on the hammer. Most terrible of all, the blue eyes were still there, staring from the severed skull.

Talli swung the hammer wildly through the air. "Stay away from me!" she shouted.

"Ms. McAlister," Volker said. "I truly wish you no harm. In fact, I'm offering you a great gift. You could live forever, and be as young and beautiful as you wish."

"Oh yeah? Isn't that what you promised Samantha?"

"As I said, a tragic case. But think of it; you could be anyone you want, look any way you want. Who would not give up everything for that?"

"I like who I am," Talli said.

"Then be yourself," Volker said. "Only better."

"I don't want to change."

"I thought we had agreed that there would be no more lies between us," he said. "Everyone wants to change. No one is happy with themselves as they are." He stepped toward her and held out his hand. "Come with me, Talli," he said. "I will show you things you never dreamed of."

Talli raised the hammer over her head. "I don't want it," she said. "I don't want any of it."

Volker sighed, a sound as loud and unreal as the sigh of an amateur actor. "I'm afraid I must insist," he said. "Join me or die, as the saying goes."

"Go to hell," Talli said. She threw the hammer with all her strength, not at Volker, but at the window that had already been broken by the chair. While the glass was still raining down, she leaped through the jagged opening.

Broken glass sliced the palms of her hands and her legs. The roof was steep and covered in snow. She dug at it, leaving patches of snow tinged pink with her blood. She skidded to a halt with her legs dangling over the edge of the roof. How high the drop was, she didn't know, and she couldn't get her head around to see.

"Again you amaze me," Volker called from the window over her head. "You would not make the mistakes of those you destroyed today. You could be like me, going on forever. Don't pass up this chance."

Talli looked up at his face. The sunlight was shining on him, and she could see his skin reddening in its glow. "You don't go on forever," she called. "You can die. Lynch did."

"I have been alive for much longer than the departed Mr. Lynch," he said. "You *can* live forever, if you are clever enough."

"No, thank you." Talli let go of the roof. She slid over the ledge and dropped.

She fell only a few feet before hitting the roof of the garage. She tried to get another grip, but the snow slid past her fingers, and she tumbled the last ten feet to the ground.

Talli lay in the snow, trying to regain her breath. She expected Volker to come strolling out the back door any moment and take her back inside, but there was no movement from the house.

The snow was cold against her bleeding hands. She got to her feet and shook the snow from her hair. Was he actually going to let her get away? Maybe he was so sure that he could catch her again that he didn't feel the need to chase her.

Talli looked at the yard. The sun was sinking low, painting the houses a deep red. The footprints that she and Alex had made the night before had been erased by the snow, but she thought she could still find the loose board, and she definitely wanted to be out of Volker's yard before dark. She started across the yard.

When the ground began to sag under Talli's feet, she didn't understand at first what had happened. With the next step, the ground sank even farther. Twenty feet away, something popped under the snow. Talli stopped, looking on in bewilderment as another puff of snow appeared ahead of her. She took another step, and the ground caved in under her feet. Only then did she remember the swimming pool.

She pushed against the collapsing plastic cover and leaped for the edge. Her fingers found a temporary grip on the lip of the pool, but it was coated with snow. Her fingers lost their hold, and she tumbled from the top, falling backward and striking her head against the bare concrete bottom of the empty pool. A lightning bolt of pain flashed across Talli's skull. She sat up slowly and looked around.

The pool cover had torn open at one corner. Now that it was loose, it was slowly tearing farther along one side under the weight of the snow. She had fallen in near the middle, at a place where it was perhaps seven feet deep. The pool sloped both up and down from where she sat, but both ends were buried in shadow.

Something moved in the shadows.

Talli got up quickly and backed against the wall. She stood in the center of the widening spot of daylight. "Who's there?" she called.

Gray forms moved at the edge of the light. "Help us," said a voice. "We're trapped here."

Talli squinted, trying to make out the form. "Come into the light," she said.

The figure moved back into the darkness. "Help us," it said again.

Talli stretched her hand up the wall behind her. She could just reach the top, but there was no way she could pull herself out. Somewhere in the pool, there had to be a ladder. But wherever it was, it was in the dark.

Another figure came forward. "Talli? Talli! It's me."

Talli took a step toward the shadowy form. "Cheryl?"

"Yes!" The figure stood back in the gloom, but Talli could make out enough of a silhouette to believe that it was Cheryl Fellini—one of the first students missing from school.

"You don't know how terrible it's been, Talli," Cheryl whined. "He took me out of the school and put me down here. He did it to all of us. Please help us, Talli."

"Come into the light," Talli repeated.

"I can't. I'm . . . sick. Help us."

Talli bit her lip. "I don't know what to do, Cheryl. How can I help?"

"Just come over here, Talli. Come into the

dark where we can talk." There was something more than pleading in her voice now. There was hunger.

Another pin gave loose, and the tear in the pool cover widened. The area of sunlight grew, and the shadowy figures scurried back. "Help us!" called another voice.

With a snap, a whole side of the pool ripped open. There were screams as the people of the shadows ran for the one remaining corner of darkness. At the end of the pool, near that puddle of black, Talli saw the sun glint redly against the metal of a ladder.

She walked toward it, keeping her eye on the dark area. The sunlight was fading fast. Any minute now, the sun would drop out of view. The figures seemed to know that. They crowded the edge of the light as if restlessly testing the edge of their prison.

"Talli!" Cheryl's voice called again. "Wait for me. I'll come with you."

Talli reached the ladder and put a foot on the first rung. "How many of you are there?" she asked.

"Not many," Cheryl said. "A couple. A few. Wait for us, Talli. I'll come out in just a second."

"You stay here," Talli said as she ascended the ladder. "I'll send help for you."

"No!" Cheryl lunged forward, reaching up. Her face split in a snarl as she snatched at Talli's foot. Then she screamed in pain and fell back into the darkness, beating at the flames that had broken out on her arms and face.

Talli reached the top of the ladder and stepped onto the snow. A coldness came over her that had nothing to do with the weather. She walked over to the pool cover and pulled. The figures below were people that she knew. Some of them had been her friends for years. But they weren't her friends anymore. She wasn't even sure they were still people.

She gave a second tug, and the cover let go completely. The last bit of darkness disappeared as Talli let the pool cover fall.

Howls and screams rose up from the pool. Burning hands reached the top of the ladder, and Talli smashed them under her boot. Smoke rose from below, trailing up into the winter sky in an oily, billowing cloud.

Talli stood by until there was no noise from the pool but the crackle of flames, then she turned and walked to the fence. It took her several tries to find the loose board. She had to dig some of the drifted snow away before she could pull it open.

She was halfway through when Volker called out to her again. "Last chance, Ms. McAlister. Will you come back and discuss this situation with me rationally?"

Talli pushed through the gap in the boards and into the narrow space between the yards.

She was halfway home when the sun dipped below the horizon. For a few seconds, the light lingered in the tops of the trees. Then it was gone, and the whole world went dark.

Twenty

Talli did not run. She knew better than to think that she could escape from Volker through speed. She had seen how fast he could move. If he wanted to run her down, he would do it.

She squeezed through the snow-choked gap between fence and shrubs and emerged in her own yard. There was a light on in the house. It looked incredibly warm and comforting in the darkness. As Talli walked toward the door, the cloak of shock that had blanketed her emotions began to drop away. The impact of what had happened in the last few hours made itself felt.

Lisa was gone. She couldn't remember when she had become friends with Lisa. It was so long ago, before they started grade school. Now Lisa was gone.

Lisa wasn't the only one. Volker had surely

taken care of Alex by now. So many faces that Talli had known for years had vanished in flames in the pool, or gone to feed Volker's monstrous hunger.

It wasn't over. Volker would be coming for Talli now, coming to kill her or make her over in his own image. She didn't think she would have long to wait.

By the time she reached the door, Talli was shaking so badly that turning the knob was an effort. She stepped into the house and closed the door. With trembling fingers, she unbuttoned her coat and let it drop to the kitchen floor. The warmth of the house reawakened the pain in her cut knees and hands.

What do I do now?

Volker was coming. Could she bolt the doors against him? In legends, vampires needed an invitation to come into a home.

There were many things about Volker that didn't match the legend of vampires, but there were many more that did. Maybe she would be safe as long as she stayed inside.

But what if she wasn't? Volker was coming. Was there anything in the house that she could use as a weapon? He hadn't answered her question about crosses and holy water. Not that she would have either in the house. Talli's family wasn't much into religion. But she ought to be able to make something. She stepped out of the kitchen and headed for her room.

201

She was surprised to see a fire crackling in the fireplace in the living room. "Dad?" she whispered. The fireplace was usually the exclusive domain of her father.

"Tallibeth!" Her mother came around the bar at the other side of the living room. "I've been so worried about you. Where have you been?"

Talli blinked. "I had to go to the school," she said. Her tongue felt thick and numb. "Are you feeling better?" she asked.

"Absolutely. Whatever I had, it seems to be gone." Mrs. McAlister looked down at Talli's torn pants. "What happened?" she said. "You better let me take a look at that."

"I just slipped and fell in the snow, Mom. I'll be okay." *Until the vampire comes to kill me*, her mind added. *I'll be just fine until he kills me.*

"Well, you'd better get up to the bathroom and wash out those cuts," said her mother. "Come back down when you're done, and we'll see about finding something to eat."

Talli nodded and headed for the stairs. She took a good grip on the banister. Her legs felt as though they might give out at any moment. She stumbled into the bathroom, ran warm water in the sink, and washed the dirt and broken glass from her hands. She glanced at herself in the mirror and saw that her face was so pale that the freckles on the bridge of her nose shone out. Looking in the mirror reminded her uncomfortably of Samantha seated at her vanity. Talli turned quickly away.

In her bedroom, she was mocked by the lurid covers of a hundred paperbacks and the posters that lined her walls. Vampires were everywhere. Dracula with his upraised cape, modern vampires baring their fangs.

Volker is coming. Talli picked through the contents of her desk, looking for something she could turn into a cross. She found nothing more substantial than Popsicle sticks and tape. She used them.

In some of the old movies, it was the faith behind the object that gave it power. If it was faith in vampires that was required, Talli had all the faith in the world. If it was faith that the cross would be able to do something, she was in serious trouble.

She heard the sound of the door downstairs and froze. *He's here,* she thought, winding a last strip of tape around her makeshift cross. Talli turned and walked out of her room.

"Talli?" called a voice from downstairs. "Where are you, honey?"

"Dad!" she shouted. She ran down the stairs two at a time. Her father was standing just inside the door, his suitcase still dangling from his hand. Talli ran to him and threw her arms around him. "Oh, Dad, I'm glad you're home!"

"Wow," he said with a chuckle. "I don't think I've gotten a greeting like that since you were six."

Mrs. McAlister beamed at him from across

203

the room. "I think it's been a hard week for Tallibeth," she said.

Talli looked up at him. She hardly knew how to begin. "Dad, there's something terrible going on," she said.

His smile faded. "Are you okay?"

"I'm okay, but Lisa is gone. I mean, she's missing. And so are lots of other kids. And I know who's behind it."

Her father took her hand in his and squeezed. "All right, honey, let me get my stuff in, and you can tell me all about it."

Volker is coming, said the persistent voice in her mind. *Go away*, she told it. *My father's here.*

He dropped the suitcase and turned back to the door. "Oh, I almost forgot," he said. "We have a visitor." He leaned out the door. "Come on in."

Volker stepped up to the door with a smile. "Thank you," he said. He slid past her father and stepped into the house.

"Hello, Ms. McAlister," he said. "It's time we finished our talk."

Talli felt her heart hitch and stop. The room did a half-spin, and then her heart started beating again, pounding out at double time. "Dad!" she shouted. "It's him, he's behind all the trouble!"

Her father smiled at her. "How interesting," he said. "Let me go get my other suitcase." He stepped out into the darkness.

Talli's mother came bustling over to Volker. "How nice to see you again," she said. "Can I get you anything?"

Volker settled himself on the couch. "I think I'll kill your daughter," he said. "And when I'm finished with that, perhaps I'll kill you, too."

"Well, I'll go check the fridge," said Mrs. McAlister. She walked out of the room.

It's happened, thought Talli. *I've flipped out completely.*

"You see how simple it is?" Volker asked. "I can tell them anything, and they won't get upset. I can order them to do something, and they'll do it."

Talli stepped back and bumped against the bar. "They're my parents," she said.

"They're nothing. They don't have the talent, and they don't have the capacity for it that you do." He stretched his arms out along the back of the couch. "Now that you have destroyed Mr. Lynch, and all my little fledglings from Westerberg, I'm in even greater need of companionship. Can I not persuade you to come with me?"

Talli walked around the end of the bar, getting it between herself and Volker. She suddenly remembered the wooden crucifix in her hands and held it up before her face. "Get out of here," she said.

Volker looked at the crude wooden cross and laughed. "Is it arts and crafts week already?" he

205

said. "Really, Ms. McAlister, you can't expect me to be impressed with a thing like that."

Mr. McAlister came back through the door with his other suitcase. "Dad!" Talli called. "He's a killer. Stop him!"

She thought she saw a flash of recognition pass through her father's eyes, but if it was there, it was gone in an instant. "We'll talk as soon as I've settled down, hon," he said. "Just let me unpack my things." He walked back past Talli, taking his suitcase upstairs, and leaving her alone with Volker.

Volker glanced at a nonexistent watch. "In any case," he said. "I'm afraid that my remaining time in this town is limited. Everyone in Westerberg will wake up tomorrow without remembering much about a Principal Volker, or the events of this past week, and I'll be moving on to the next place."

"I'll remember," Talli said.

"Yes," he said. "You will if you're alive. Will you be, Talli? This is the final question. Do you come with me and live, or do I kill you, and take your parents for dessert?"

The wooden cross fell from Talli's hands and smacked on the floor. "Leave my parents alone," she said.

"I'll be happy to, if you'll come with me."

Talli's eye fell on something on the bar, a tiny thing behind the empty ice bucket. She picked it up and cupped it in the palm of her hand.

"If you promise to leave my parents alone," she said. "I'll come with you."

"Excellent!" Volker said. "You'll not regret it. I can show you things you've never seen. Believe me, the world can change a lot in a few centuries—you'll never have to worry about being bored."

"What . . . what do I have to do?" she said.

Volker stood and stretched out his hands to her. "Come to me," he said. "Come to me and be blessed by the gift of youth and power."

Talli hesitated. She ran a finger along the curved metal of the object in her hand, then jammed it into the back pocket of her jeans, and walked across the room to Volker.

His face was young again, smooth and un-lined. He looked no more than twenty. His short hair was jet-black. "Just take my hands," he said.

Talli did.

His grip was firm. "This is a sacred thing," he said to her. He put his mouth close to the top of her head, his words puffing against her red hair. His fingers folded over hers like a vise, and she felt something sweep into her, over her, through her. It was a tide of power and life, a well of strength that made her want to dance. She threw her head back, and with her eyes closed she could feel the power moving across her like a thousand electric ants. Her hair rose around her head in a red nimbus.

This isn't evil, she thought. *How can this be*

207

bad? But then she felt the black thread at the heart of the power, a current of greed and self-ishness that lived only to feed. It was a hunger that could only be fed by drawing in the lives of other people. That was the real root of Volker's blessing, the true nature of his power—undying hunger.

She wanted to pull away, or at least part of her did. But the flow of energy was too strong, too sweet. Even with the bitter core, it felt too good to give up. There were flashes of light in it, pieces and fragments of memory. Talli pulled it all in, feeling it surge and swirl inside her.

"Now," whispered Volker. "Now we really begin."

The flow of power doubled and redoubled. Talli could feel the force of the lives passing over her. Each one had a texture, a distinct quality. She experienced a thousand things in a flash, bits of lives that spread out over a span of centuries. She saw things, heard things, felt things that all the people Volker had taken this power from had experienced.

Lisa.

Talli's eyes snapped open. In that maelstrom of lives and memories, she had felt something as familiar as her own face. She had felt Lisa's life run through her. Volker had built his power from a patchwork of souls, and one of them had been Lisa's. Talli looked up at Volker's face. His head was tilted far back, and his eyes were clenched tightly shut. Veins stood out in his neck, and he shook with the power that was running through him.

"Now we will share the secret source," he said. "The power that runs through my heart. And when you have sampled it, we will be as one."

Talli felt a fringe of it, something both black and bright, beautiful and terrible. Then she pulled her hands free. Blue sparks crossed the gap between Talli and Volker. For Talli, the feeling was like being electrocuted—the muscles in her arms and legs jerked and danced of their own accord, leaping at each crack of the blue light.

Black fire trailed over her skin, and her hair rose in a red cloud around her face. She managed to get one hand behind her back, and fumbled out the thing she had taken from the bar. In the middle of Volker's fire, it felt as cold as ice.

Volker opened his eyes and looked at her. "What are you doing?" he said. Sparks jumped between his teeth as he spoke. "We are not finished."

"We're finished," Talli said, and she drove the object into the exposed flesh of his throat.

Lightning snapped around Volker in a halo of writhing blue power. He reached for the thing in his throat, but crackling bolts knocked his hands away.

There was an awful squealing in the room, the sound of dreadful energies fleeing into the air. Volker's body twisted in a ball of light. His hands flowed, becoming first the hands of a woman, then an old man, then a child. Every feature of his face went through similar gyrations. "Help me," he moaned.

He fell back onto the carpet, bucking and bouncing like the girl who had had a fit at school. As the light guttered, it seemed to Talli that Volker's form began to shrink, and the shapes he took were less well defined. His face looked like something a child had created from lumps of clay, with empty holes for eyes and a mouth that was a toothless scream. His hands became fingerless masses.

Talli did not turn away. She watched it all. For the sake of all those Volker had killed, she watched every moment of his death.

He continued to shrink and lose shape. When his head disappeared into the open collar of his dress shirt, it was no more than an eyeless lump. A few minutes later, the last flickers of blue lightning ran up and down his pale gray suit. They left nothing behind but the singed clothing, and a strong smell of burned flesh.

Talli stood there for a long time. There had been too many tricks, too many false hopes for her to believe it was really over. It wasn't until a buzzer went off in the kitchen that she stepped away from the smoking clothes.

Talli found her mother asleep at the kitchen table. There was a roast in the oven. She turned it off, and went to look for her father.

He was asleep too, spread out and snoring on the bed beside his unopened suitcase.

Talli went back downstairs, walked into the living room, and stood over the empty suit. She hoped that when her parents woke, they wouldn't remember any of this. She began to cry again for everything that had happened, but this time, her sadness was mingled with relief. Whatever had happened, at least it was over.

She bent and picked up a shiny object from the floor. It was a corkscrew, nothing but a corkscrew. Talli had given it to her parents as a present on their twenty-fifth wedding anniversary. She held it close to her eyes and saw the words that she knew would be there: "Sterling Silver."

Sometimes, the legends were true.

Talli sat down on the couch and rocked back and forth, crying softly while her parents slept.

Epilogue

❧

Sunday

The men who searched the house did a very good job. He was lucky it was night. There was no doubt they would have found him in the daylight, and if they had found him, he knew he would be dead.

That was almost all he did know. Most of his memory was locked under a muddy swirl of pain. Even trying to think was agony.

He knew these things: stay out of the sunlight, sunlight is dangerous; stay away from people, people are dangerous; feed the hunger, the hunger is your master. Those were the things he knew, and those were all the things he needed to know.

He came back to the house after the men

had left. There was a gnawing pain in his gut; a hunger he was not even sure how to feed. But it was not too strong. Yet. He could put it off for now, put it off till the next night. First he had to find someplace to spend the searing hours of daylight.

The men had taken almost everything from the house. Evidence. The word floated in his mind. He did not know what it meant. Perhaps later he would remember. Now there was only the end of the night, and the coming of the sun.

He found a place. It was an ideal place: cool, dry, and absolutely without light.

He closed his eyes and rested.

In the cellar of the house that had been Volker's, under the lid of the old meat locker, Alex waited for night to fall.

ABOUT THE AUTHOR

M. C. Sumner lives out in the country, in a town even smaller than Westerberg. His house is perched precariously on the side of a hill, and he is the proud owner of one of the ugliest patches of woods in several states. Like many writers, he keeps a menagerie of animals, with current residents that include an iguana, a giant day gecko, an African house snake, a tank of fish, several mice, and one very spoiled golden retriever.

In addition to this trilogy and his previous book, *Deadly Stranger*, he has sold a number of short stories. His stories have appeared in *Isaac Asimov's Science Fiction* Magazine, *Tomorrow* Magazine, *Dragon* Magazine, and in a number of anthologies. He was a first-place winner in the Writers of the Future Contest.

He is currently at work on a new crop of young adult thrillers.

≛ HarperPaperbacks *By Mail*

Friends and strangers move into a beach house for an unforgettable summer of passion, conflict, and romance in the hot bestselling series

OCEAN CITY

Look for these new titles in the bestselling *Freshman Dorm* series:

#30 Freshman Temptation

#31 Freshman Fury

Super #4: Freshman Holiday

And in the tradition of *The Vampire Diaries*, now there's

DARK MOON LEGACY by Cynthia Blair.

VOLUME I
The Curse

VOLUME II
The Seduction

VOLUME III
The Rebellion